THE KAT SINCLAIR FILES

BY MICHELLE SCHUSTERMAN

DEAD AIR

Grosset & Dunlap
An Imprint of Penguin Random House

THiS ONE'S FOR THE SKELETON IN YOUR CLOSET—MS

GROSSET & DUNLAP
Penguin Young Readers Group
An Imprint of Penguin Random House LLC

Text copyright © 2015 by Michelle Schusterman. Cover illustration copyright © 2015 by Stephanie Olesh. All rights reserved. Previously published in hardcover in 2015 by Grosset & Dunlap. This paperback edition published in 2016 by Grosset & Dunlap, an imprint of Penguin Random House LLC, 345 Hudson Street, New York, New York 10014. GROSSET & DUNLAP is a trademark of Penguin Random House LLC. Printed in the USA.

Book design by Kayla Wasil

The Library of Congress has cataloged the hardcover edition under the following Control Number: 2015951115.

ISBN 9780515157154

10 9 8 7 6 5 4 3 2 1

CHAPTER ONE
THE THING

MY first real memory was hearing my grandma scream bloody murder while being attacked by zombie hamsters. That scream won her Best Actress at the Dark Cheese B-Movie Awards in 1979. It was also her standard reaction for birthday presents, hide-and-seek, touchdowns, and any other scream-worthy occasion.

So when I heard her award-winning shriek come from downstairs while I was duct-taping a box of books, I didn't even flinch. Picking up a Sharpie, I scrawled *Mysteries & Harry Potter* on the side, then tossed the marker down and left my room.

"Was it that diaper commercial again?" I asked when I

1

entered the living room. "With the creepy dancing babies?"

"Hang on, KitKat." Grandma's eyes were glued to the television. "This is the Glasgow episode, that old inn with the haunted garden. The grate scene is coming up."

I glanced at the screen and rolled my eyes. "Again? You've probably seen this a—"

But Grandma flapped a perfectly manicured hand at me, so I zipped it and sat on the armrest of her chair.

Passport to Paranormal claimed to be "the most haunted show on television." Translation: "The most low-budget ghost-hunting show ever, which blames equipment malfunctions on paranormal activity." During the pilot episode last year, the show had blacked out for almost two minutes near the end. The network, Fright TV, couldn't explain the dead air. So naturally, the crew claimed ghosts were responsible.

Ratings weren't off the charts, but *Passport to Paranormal*'s small group of fans were pretty intense. They had a website and forums with heated debates over each episode, plus lots of gossip about the cast of *P2P*. They sold merchandise, too. Grandma was currently wearing a *P2P* baseball cap that said I BELIEVE.

You never saw anything legitimately supernatural, but the show was still pretty entertaining. Besides, ghosts had nothing to do with why most fans—like Grandma— were so obsessed.

On the screen, a guy with a flashlight edged around a stone wall. He was pretty good-looking, I had to admit . . . I mean, if too-long-to-be-real eyelashes and cheekbones sharper than a knife are your idea of good-looking.

"I heard something," a female voice behind the camera whispered—Jess Capote, I knew right away. I'd never met her in person, but she and my dad went to college together. They'd both worked on the university's morning news show. "Right down there. Sam?"

Sam Sumners closed his eyes. "I feel his presence."

I snorted. Grandma swatted my arm.

"I think it's coming from the grate," whispered Jess, and Sam bent over to examine it. The camera zoomed in on the grate—and paused, just for a second, on Sam's butt.

Grandma sighed happily. "There it is."

"*Grandma!*"

"What?" She finally tore her eyes off the screen to hit pause on the remote. "That's some serious eye candy."

I groaned. "Oh my God."

"Oh my God is right," Grandma agreed, her gaze straying back to the screen.

"I don't get why everyone freaks out over him," I said, wrinkling my nose. "He looks like a Ken doll. Plastic."

Grandma pressed her hand to her heart. "You will not speak ill of Sam Sumners in my presence. And twenty bucks says you change your mind when you meet him in person."

"Doubt it." But a flash of nerves hit me anyway. Not about meeting Sam, the show's psychic medium and resident pretty boy. About being a part of *Passport to Paranormal* in general. After losing their third and most recent host, they would resume filming the second season at the end of this week with the newest host: Jack Sinclair, former anchor for

Rise and Shine, Ohio! He was also my dad.

In less than two days, Dad and I would be somewhere in the Netherlands. Instead of sleeping in my horror movie–postered bedroom, I'd be living in hotel rooms and buses. Instead of coasting through eighth grade on a steady stream of Bs at Riverview Middle School, I'd be homeschooled (or, I guess, roadschooled). Instead of hanging out with my best friends, Trish and Mark, I'd be spending most of the next year with a bunch of people who chased ghosts for a living.

Dad had given me the option to stay in Ohio with Mom. Which, to be honest, wasn't an option at all. Because of the Thing.

"How's the packing coming?" asked Grandma. I realized too late that she'd been squinting at me from under her baseball cap with her I-can-read-your-mind expression.

"I'm pretty much done," I replied. "Dad's got to weigh the bags, though—they can't be over fifty pounds."

Grandma leaned over and pulled something out from behind her armchair. "Well, I hope you have room for a little going-away present."

She held out a stuffed, wrinkled gift bag with snowmen all over it, and I laughed. We'd been recycling that bag for all gift-giving occasions since the Christmas when I was nine. It looked really festive until you realized the snowmen were zombies and the snow was spattered with blood.

My smile faded when I peered inside and spotted the DVD. "*Invasion of the Flesh-Eating Rodents*? You know I've got this already!"

"It's the latest special edition!" Grandma said defensively.

"Not officially released yet. And there's three minutes of never-before-seen footage. A guinea pig attacks me in the shower."

Flesh-Eating Rodents was "Scream Queen" Edie Mills's (aka: Grandma's) seventeenth and final movie. At age six, I watched her play a butt-kicking veterinarian who saved the day when a rabies vaccine went horrifically wrong. I kept examining her fingers while the credits rolled, marveling that I couldn't see all the chunks the hamsters had gnawed off.

She'd shown me her movies in reverse order over the next few years—as I got older, film-star Grandma got younger. My least favorite was *Vampires of New Jersey* (her hair looked freaking ridiculous). The best one was *Cannibal Clown Circus* (she played a trapeze artist whose safety net was gnawed to pieces by zombies halfway through her act). I saw her first movie, *Mutant Cheerleaders Attack*, on Thanksgiving when I was eight. Watching your teenage grandmother in a cheerleading uniform with oozing scabs all over her legs is best done after eating your cranberry-sauced turkey, not before.

"Anyway, that's not so much a gift for *you*," Grandma admitted, tapping the DVD. "I thought you might want to show it to Sam."

I tried to glare at her and failed. "Grandma. No."

"You never know, he might like what he sees." She winked coyly, smoothing back her silver-streaked hair, and I laughed. "Now look back in that bag. I think you missed something."

Eagerly, I reached in the bag again and pulled out something wrapped in tissue paper. I tore it off, and the smile froze on my face.

It was a camera. Specifically, it was the Elapse E-250 with a pancake lens, silver with a cool purple strap, the smallest and most compact digital SLR camera ever—and the exact one I'd spent most of seventh grade begging for. But that was last year, when I was still tagging along with Mom to every wedding or party she shot, drooling over all her cool professional camera equipment.

Then she moved to Cincinnati, and I stopped caring about photography.

Still . . . My hands gripped the Elapse, finger tapping the shutter button. Without really meaning to, I flipped it on and held it up to my eye. Grandma's beaming face filled the viewfinder, and I lowered the camera hastily.

"This is way too expensive," I blurted out. "I mean, thank you, but I know it's—I mean, I don't . . ."

Grandma waved a hand dismissively. "Don't start with all that. Consider this a going-away-birthday-Christmas present, all right?"

I swallowed hard. "Yes, but . . ."

But I'm not into this anymore. I don't want to be a photographer. That's what I kept trying to say, but I couldn't.

"Listen to me," Grandma said, and once again, I was pretty sure she'd read my thoughts. "You're about to go traveling the world. Not only that, you're going to hunt *ghosts*. You and your father keep calling this your big *adventure*, and I demand pictures."

"I could send you postcards," I said, flipping the mode dial with my thumb.

Grandma rolled her eyes. "What is this, the fifties? I'm not waiting by the mailbox. E-mail me. Hit me up with a text."

"Grandma," I groaned. "Stop talking like that."

"Of course, you won't be able to text from out of the country," she went on, as if I hadn't spoken. "Still, you can put them on Facebook. Or . . ." Grandma's eyes widened, and she clapped her hands. "I've got it."

I held the camera up again, touching my finger lightly to the shutter button. "What?"

"You should start a blog!"

Click!

Lowering the camera, I made a face. "I don't think so."

"Why not?" Grandma demanded.

I shrugged, examining the Elapse more closely. "I don't like writing. And a blog sounds like too much work."

"I'll tell you what's going to be too much work," she said. "Repeating the same stories over and over again when you talk to me and your friends and your mother and everyone else who'll want to know what the glamorous ghost-hunting life is like. This way you can just tell us all at once."

"Eh, I'll think about it." I chewed my lip, flipping the mode dial back and forth again. "Hey, Grandma?"

"Yes?" She was reaching for the remote when the question I'd been dying to ask for weeks now finally came tumbling out.

"Is Mom back in Chelsea?"

Grandma's hand froze over the remote, and her mouth pursed slightly. "What makes you think that?"

My stomach plummeted. I'd been hoping for *No, of course not!* "Trish," I said, trying to sound casual. "Her brother said she was at the Starbucks by his school a few weeks ago. And she thought she saw her at the mall last weekend, too," I added. Actually, Trish had been positive. *"No one besides you and your mom has that crazy-long hair, Kat."*

Grandma rewound the grate scene, chewing her lip a little. She seemed to be waiting for me to say something else. Or maybe she was just stalling, trying to think of a lie. Not that Grandma would ever lie to me. Neither would Dad. They both knew better.

"Anyway, I thought maybe she came back to . . . say good-bye to us, or something," I finished lamely. Sighing, Grandma settled back in her chair and looked at me.

"If you want to know what your mother's up to, maybe it's time you start taking her calls."

She didn't say it meanly, but I reeled a little bit. Grandma reached out to pat my hand, and I jerked it away.

"Never mind," I said shortly. "It doesn't matter, anyway. I've got to finish packing."

Without looking at Grandma, I hurried back upstairs and closed my bedroom door. My oversize, must-weigh-less-than-fifty-pounds megabackpack was propped up against my wardrobe, stuffed with T-shirts, jeans, and hoodies. Most of my other stuff was in boxes for storage, although my furniture was staying put. That was the nice thing about having Grandma as a landlady—she would just rent this place to new tenants until Dad and I came home, so I didn't have to say good-bye to the house I grew up in.

Although to be honest, a small part of me didn't care if I ever saw it again.

I knelt down next to one of the storage boxes. This one was filled with sundresses I hated. The Thing crouched next to me, radiating disapproval as I taped the box closed. I ignored it.

I'd almost told Grandma about the Thing probably a hundred times, but I knew she'd never believe it existed. In *The Monster in Her Closet*, Grandma played a girl whose childhood imaginary friend Edgar was terrorizing her neighborhood, and no one believed her.

The Thing was kind of like Edgar. I couldn't prove it existed. But that didn't mean it wasn't real.

For a few minutes, I tried to distract myself by taping and labeling boxes. It didn't work, though. There was no way Trish had mistaken someone else for my mom—we'd grown up in each other's houses; she knew what my mother looked like as well as I did. And her hair—our hair, I guess—*was* pretty hard to miss. The superlong thick braid suddenly felt heavy against my back.

It was the only feature Mom and I shared. She was pale in winter and fake-tanned in summer, with Grandma's dark blue eyes and tiny nose. My skin and eyes were the same shades of brown as Dad's, and our noses were both a little on the longish side. But Mom and I had the same slightly coarse, brown-black hair that fell in waves down to our waists. Two summers ago at the beach, I'd begged her to let me chop it off, but she'd said I'd regret it. What I really regretted were the hours I spent trying to get out all the saltwater knots and tangles.

Grabbing the scissors, I cut a strip of tape a little more viciously than necessary and slapped it on a box of dressy shoes. Then I marched over to my dresser and set the tape and scissors down next to the Elapse.

It really was an awesome camera. But I didn't want to be a photographer anymore.

My fingers tightened around the scissors.

Maybe I didn't want long hair anymore, either.

Suddenly, my heart was pounding loud and fast in my ears. With one hand, I pulled my braid over my shoulder. With the other, I held the scissors to it at about shoulder level. Then I slid them an inch higher. And then another . . . and another.

Then I started cutting.

It took longer than I expected, probably half a minute of hacking away. When I finished, I set my braid down on my dresser and stared at it. It was weird, kind of like looking at my own severed arm (but obviously not as gross). Then I looked in the mirror.

My hair was *short*. And slanted, since I'd cut it over one shoulder. I used a comb to part it down the center. Then I trimmed the left side until it was as short as the right and examined my reflection.

It was about chin-length, and really choppy. My head felt a lot lighter. I liked it.

I went back to packing, whistling the *Passport to Paranormal* theme song as I worked.

CHAPTER TWO
THE CURSE OF THE
STALE MUFFINS

From: acciopancakes@mymail.net
To: trishhhhbequiet@mymail.net
Subject: Re: DON'T LEAVE ME!!!

Trish,
Am at airport. Guessing Plan Frogpocalypse was a fail. Also a
fail: waking up at 4 a.m. Our cab came at 4:30, and me and Dad
were both still asleep. Oops.
Kat

"I'M sorry, Mr. Sinclair. This is more than a pound over
the limit."

"No problem."

Dad's talk-show host smile was going strong this
morning. The airport check-in lady smiled back and
watched, along with me and the approximately four
zillion people behind us in line, as he unzipped my
bulging megabackpack and started rummaging inside.

"Dad—"

"I got it, Kat," he said. "It's all just a matter of weight
distribution."

I glanced at the line. A couple of blond girls, both

younger than me, clutched the handles of their bright pink suitcases. Their parents were right behind them, the mom balancing a little boy on her hip.

"Mickey!" the kid shrieked, and his mom smiled.

"Mickey!" she agreed, stifling a yawn. "We're going to meet Mickey tomorrow!"

"Assuming we actually make this flight," her husband grumbled, shooting Dad a dirty look.

Family of five kicking off fall break with a trip to Disney World. How lovely for them.

I turned back around to face Dad, who was holding up my puffy blue parka in one hand and a giant baggie stuffed with underwear and socks in the other. A green plaid bra was pressed up at the front like a kid's face smooshed in a candy-store window.

"Dad!" I hissed, and he tossed me the parka.

"Don't know what I was thinking!" Kneeling, he unzipped the already-stuffed duffel bag at his feet and crammed the baggie inside. "Jackets don't count as carry-ons; we can just take them on board with us."

Dad pulled his own black parka out of my backpack (he'd run out of room in his), and we watched the scale drop from 51.2 to 50.5.

"Almost there," the check-in lady said encouragingly. Behind us, Blond Dad groaned.

"Sorry, folks." Dad beamed at the line of bleary-eyed travelers, and a few smiled back feebly. "Just another second."

He started groping around the backpack again, and the

check-in lady cautiously peered inside.

"What about that jar?"

Dad turned to me, and I swallowed hard.

"A jar of sand is pretty heavy," the check-in lady added, her face suddenly uncertain as she glanced from Dad to me.

Dad lifted the jar out of my backpack. The three of us had been bringing it to the lake every summer since I could remember, adding a little more sand every time. It had been Mom's idea. I was in charge of packing it for every vacation—I hadn't thought twice about bringing the jar. Dad cleared his throat. "What do you think, Kat?"

"It's just sand," I said with a shrug. "Leave it."

Dad nodded slowly. "Okay. If you're sure."

"Perfect!" the check-in lady chirped, and I saw that the weight had dropped to 49.6. "Now you're ready to fly."

She set the jar under her console as we picked up our stuff, and I wondered what she'd do with it. Throw it away, I figured. She probably thought we were weirdos, trying to bring a jar of dirt to Europe.

Once we'd made it through the crazy-long security line and the crazier-long Starbucks line, Dad and I flopped gratefully into a pair of black plastic chairs. I devoured two day-old blueberry muffins in about a minute. Dad burned his tongue chugging his latte and said it was worth it.

"This hair's freaking me out," he said, making little circles in the air as he pointed at my head. "I could've taken you to a barber, you know."

I was trying to pick the blueberries out of my teeth. "It was a last-minute decision."

"Mmm." Dad stirred his coffee, eyeing me. "You didn't leave all that hair in your room, did you? It'll scare the new tenants."

"Grandma took it," I told him. "She said she'd donate it to some organization that makes wigs for cancer patients."

Dad smiled. "That's nice, Kat."

"Hey, want to see something cool?" I asked.

"Of course."

"I need your laptop."

After a few minutes of trying to get his clunky old laptop to connect to the airport's Wi-Fi, I opened the browser, typed in a URL, then turned the screen to face Dad. His eyebrows shot up.

"The Kat Sinclair Files?"

"It's a blog!" I said. "It was Grandma's idea. This way I can post stories about the haunted places we visit for her and Trish and Mark and . . . anyone else. Plus pictures and stuff like that, too."

Dad laughed. "Very Nancy Drew."

"And Hardy Boys," I agreed, thinking sadly of all the boxes of books I'd left in storage.

"Ladies and gentlemen, we'll begin boarding flight 221 to New York in just a few minutes."

A rush of nervous excitement flooded through me. Now that we were actually at the airport, this whole thing felt more *real*. When Mom took off last spring, I was convinced she'd come back. After all, she'd done this twice before—once when I was five, and again a few years later. Both times, she returned in less than two weeks, full of apologies and new promises.

Not this time, though. Two weeks passed, then three. A month later, she was still in Cincinnati.

That's when things got weird. By the time school let out, I'd realized Mom probably wasn't coming back. But I was still in a constant state of anticipation, waiting for something I knew logically wasn't going to happen. And Dad started acting . . . restless. Like he needed a distraction, but nothing worked—not our traditional summer-slasher movie marathons, not a nighttime visit to Chelsea's one and only supposedly haunted house, not even a visit to the paranormal museum on the other side of town. When I started school in August, Dad decided he was bored at *Rise and Shine, Ohio!* and started looking for anchor jobs at other networks, in other cities. After a few weeks, he posted something about job-hunting on his college's alumni Facebook page, and Jess Capote left a comment:

P2P *needs a new host! Want to chase ghosts with me? ;)*

I still wasn't sure if Jess had been kidding around. For all I knew, she was just as shocked as I was when Dad replied: *Yes!*

"An adventure, Kat!" he'd said in a hyperenthusiastic sort of way, already looking up plane-ticket prices. "Traveling all over the world . . . It'll be an experience, visiting all these new places. *Haunted* places," he added, beaming. "That's where the best stories are, right? The haunted places."

He went on and on like that. But I understood what he really meant. Yesterday at the going-away party my art teacher had given me, everyone kept asking about all the places I was *going*. And all I could think about was that I was finally *leaving*.

I mean, I loved my house, school was easy enough. And I'd definitely miss Trish and Mark, and Grandma, of course. But I still wanted to go. It felt like an escape. I knew Dad must feel the same way.

And secretly, I was hoping maybe the Thing would stay in Chelsea.

"If the plane has Wi-Fi, I might work on my blog," I told Dad when the other passengers started boarding. "I bet I can find a cooler layout."

"Sure." Dad took a final swig of his coffee and tossed the paper cup into the trash can next to his chair. "I'm sleeping the whole flight. And the one after that." He groaned, stretching his arms over his head. "And the one after that. Two layovers, bleargh."

I bounced up and down, watching the line of first-class people form at the gate. "I don't know how you can even think about sleeping," I told him. But ten minutes after the seat-belt light went off, I was crashed out, facedown on the laptop before the drink cart even rolled by.

CHAPTER THREE

THE BOY WITH NO EYES

Post: Travel Is a Beating
Seriously, all I want is a shower and a bed.

THAT was my first blog post. No pictures, nothing else. I wrote it in Munich during our second layover. I didn't think anyone needed to hear the details of the almost eighteen hours of boarding and unboarding I'd endured—squinting at airport maps, dragging luggage from gate to gate, chewing insanely dry turkey sandwiches, and kneeing the backs of inconsiderate people who insisted on reclining their seats into my lap before the plane even took off.

When Dad and I finally checked in to our motel in Rotterdam, I passed out face-first on one of the twin beds and slept so hard not even Dad's chainsaw-snores woke me.

RING-RING. RING-RING.

I groped around without opening my eyes, wondering why my alarm sounded so weird. Then I heard Dad's groggy voice.

"'Lo? This is Jack . . ." He cleared his voice, suddenly

sounding much more awake. "Lidia, hello! Yes, we're up. Half an hour? Sounds good, see you soon!"

"Why'd they call in the middle of the night?" I mumbled. Dad pulled open the curtains and I yelped, ducking under the blanket to shield my eyes from the evil sunshine.

"It's almost eleven," Dad said. "That was the producer— I'm going to check out the entrance to Crimptown, where we're filming." He yanked the blanket from my face. "Haunted tunnels, pirate ghosts . . . you coming?"

My response was a grunt. I flipped over, piling two pillows on top of my head.

But I couldn't go back to sleep, despite my grainy, tired eyes. By the time Dad got out of the shower, I'd dug some clean jeans and a *Tales from the Crypt* T-shirt from my megabackpack.

"Two minutes," I promised, ducking around him and into the bathroom.

Fifteen minutes later, we were out the door, the tangy smell of saltwater slapping me in the face. A man in a suit whizzed past us on a bicycle, jacket slung over his shoulder. I watched him head off the boardwalk toward the skyscrapers to our left. Farther down the harbor, I saw a massive bridge arched over the river, dozens of cables sweeping up from one end and connecting to a white, geometric sort of tower. It was oddly graceful-looking.

"The Erasmus Bridge," Dad told me. "Beautiful, isn't it? They call it the Swan."

I nodded without responding. My head felt like someone had stuffed it with cotton balls, but through the fuzz, realization was starting to dawn.

I was in another country.

I followed Dad mutely down the wide boardwalk, eavesdropping on conversations and not recognizing a single word. Dad and I had listened to a Learn Conversational Dutch app he'd downloaded on one of our flights. Apparently nothing had sunk in through my jet-lagged stupor.

Suddenly, I was very aware of how far from Chelsea I was, like someone had just swooped me from Ohio to this spot in two seconds flat. It was exciting and terrifying, like one of those elevator-drop rides at an amusement park. The breeze ruffled my newly cropped hair, and I felt a rush of giddiness. Maybe I really had escaped the Thing.

"Do you see Jess?" I asked.

"Lidia's meeting us, actually," Dad replied, his eyes scanning the crowd. "Jess is with the rest of the crew."

My stomach rumbled loudly. "Are we going to have breakfast with them? Do you think they have pancakes in the Netherl—"

"Jack?"

Dad and I both turned to face a woman barely taller than me. The frames of her glasses were huge and bright blue, the lenses magnifying her amber eyes. Strands of frizzy dark hair that had come loose from her ponytail whipped around her face in the wind. She looked kind of frazzled, but her smile was warm and friendly.

"Lidia!" Dad turned on the talk-show charm full force. "Great to finally meet you."

They shook hands, and then Lidia held her hand out to

me. "You must be Kat. Lidia Bettencourt."

"Nice to meet you, Ms. Bettencourt," I said, taking her hand gingerly. It felt frail, like I might snap a bone if I squeezed a little too hard.

"Oh, just Lidia, please!" Rummaging in her purse, Lidia frowned. "Now, let's see, I thought I . . . here!" She pulled out an odd-looking gadget I recognized from watching the show—an EMF meter, which was supposed to . . . well, I wasn't entirely sure how they worked. Grandma called them *spook sensors*. "Nope, that's not it . . ." After another few seconds of groping around her bag, Lidia pulled out a few granola bars with a triumphant "Aha!" and held one out to me.

"Thanks!" I said eagerly, ripping the wrapper off and devouring half in one bite.

Dad took the other bar, watching me in amusement. "We haven't had a chance to eat breakfast yet," he told Lidia.

"I figured," Lidia said. "Jet lag is brutal, but don't worry—you'll get used to it. So, the theater's just a few blocks . . . You don't mind walking?"

"Not a bit!" Dad replied cheerfully. I trailed behind them most of the way along the waterfront, staring out at the boats and wishing I had about eight more granola bars.

Ten minutes later, we were looking up at a ramshackle theater. The bulbs around the marquee had all been removed, and only three letters were still hanging on—an *I*, an *O*, and a crooked *U*. The box office was boarded up and covered in faded graffiti.

"Very creepy." Dad said it like a compliment.

"What's with the 'IOU'?" I asked, pointing at the marquee.

Lidia tilted her head.

"Ooh, I hadn't noticed that," she replied. "Good eye! Remind me to point it out to Jess—we should get a shot of it for the opening sequence."

I stared at the marquee again and found myself mentally framing it, adjusting the focus . . . Then I shook my head. I'd left the Elapse in my suitcase intentionally.

"Do you believe in ghosts, Kat?"

Startled, I looked at Lidia. She was smiling at me. "Oh, um . . . I don't know."

"Good answer," Lidia said with a grin. "I'll ask you again in a week or so. Maybe your answer will be different."

"Maybe." I couldn't keep the doubt out of my voice.

"We'll fill you in on the Crimptown story during the meeting," Lidia said to Dad. "I've got a few people lined up tomorrow for you to interview. There are a couple of entrances to Crimptown, but the theater's got the entrance where the official tour starts, so that's where we've set up camp for now." She turned to me again. "Kat, I hope you don't mind hanging out for an hour or two while we get your dad settled in. My nephew's here, so he can keep you company. We're *so* glad this homeschool thing worked out with the two of you."

I blinked a few times. "Um . . . what?"

"I actually haven't filled Kat in on that yet," Dad cut in, shooting me an apologetic look.

"Filled me in on what?"

"Oh, it's my fault—this was all so last minute," Lidia said quickly. "My nephew, Oscar—he's your age—he's been asking if I could take custody of him since last winter. He's been with my sister in Oregon, but he . . . well, he had some problems at his school. But I'm always on the road—I couldn't just pull him out of school altogether . . ." She paused for breath, beaming at Dad. "Then Jess found us a new host with a thirteen-year-old daughter! And Jack said—"

"He's homeschooling me," I interrupted. "Right?"

"That was the initial plan," Dad said quickly. "But Lidia came up with a better idea."

"We have an intern," Lidia rushed on. "Her name's Mi Jin, she graduated last May—college, not high school!—and we asked her if she'd be willing to tutor you *and* Oscar since she'll be less involved with the show than your dad and I, and she'd have more time. Plus, you know, a little extra cash in her pocket."

My mouth opened and closed soundlessly. Lidia talked so fast it was hard to keep up. "Hang on," I sputtered. "So this guy's mom let him come with you just because he doesn't like his school?"

"No, no, his mother died years ago," Lidia said. "He's my brother's son, and . . ." She paused, then waved her hand dismissively. "It's a long story. Anyway, let's get in there so you can meet everyone! Kat, I hope you can tag along tomorrow for your dad's interviews; there's a pretty cool story behind Crimptown . . ."

I tuned her out as she led the way into the theater. So I had a new teacher *and* a new classmate. That could be interesting.

The inside of the theater didn't look too bad. It was chilly and dim and pretty run-down, but it wasn't falling apart or covered in mold or anything like that. But this was just the entrance to Crimptown, the focus for this episode. All I knew was that it was a tunnel system beneath the Rotterdam waterfront that was supposedly haunted by the ghost of a pirate. And tomorrow we would spend the night down there.

Not that I was scared or worried or anything—growing up watching horror movies starring my grandmother helped me develop an immunity to creepy stuff. (Like the kissing scenes. Oh God, the kissing scenes were the *worst*. You haven't experienced real horror until you've watched your grandmother make out with a vampire.)

As we passed the small bar in the lobby, I heard the low murmur of people talking. Lidia opened the door to the box office and gestured for me to enter. The chatter stopped, and several heads turned in my direction.

"Hi!" I said brightly, doing my best Anchor Dad impression. "I'm Kat Sinclair, your new host." In my mind, I could hear Trish and Mark snickering. Of course they weren't actually here, so my stupid nonjoke was greeted with silence and raised eyebrows. Sighing, I stepped aside to let Dad in.

Soon everyone was shaking hands, and all sorts of names were flying around. I hung back, trying to figure out who was who.

Of course Sam Sumners was easy to spot. Somehow, he looked even more plastic in real life than on TV—shiny black hair, crayon-blue eyes, and eyelashes straight out of a mascara commercial. He smiled at me, and I imagined Grandma swooning and tried not to snicker.

Next to Sam was a scruffy-faced guy with thick eyebrows permanently arched in a way that suggested he was about to say something sarcastic—Roland Yeske, the parapsychologist. (Seriously, a psychologist specializing in the paranormal. Grandma swears it's a real profession. I have my doubts.)

I also recognized Jess Capote—bleached-blond hair and a gazillion freckles—just before she threw her arms around Dad in a bear hug. Behind them, a girl with an eyebrow ring sat with her combat boots propped up on the table, toying with one of about a dozen cord bracelets. I'd only seen her in a few of the more recent episodes.

Lidia spoke up over all the chatter. "Hey, where'd my nephew get off to?"

"He said he was going up to the projection room," Roland said, tilting his chair back. He looked at me pointedly. "Did we get picked up by Nickelodeon or something? What's with all the kids?"

Jess swatted him on the back of the head. "You knew Jack was bringing his daughter," she said airily before turning to me with a broad smile. "Great to have you here, Kat! We're about to talk your dad's ear off and it's probably going to get real boring real fast, so . . ."

"She'll be fine on her own for a bit, right, Kat?" Dad smiled encouragingly at me, and I nodded.

"The theater's not all that big," Lidia added. "You probably saw the entrance to the tunnels by the bar—they still do organized tours, so stay up here. Oh, we've got a laptop set up by the projection room upstairs. The connection is slow, but you should be able to get online if you want. That's probably where Oscar is."

Roland let out a groan that sounded half-amused. "Oh God, we've got two thirteen-year-olds. This place is gonna be hormone central."

"Don't worry," I said dryly before anyone else could respond. "I'm pretty sure I can control myself."

Everyone laughed, and even Roland grinned a little. "Good to know. Nice shirt, by the way."

"*Great* shirt," the girl with the eyebrow ring said fervently. "Do you like the comics, too?"

I glanced down at my shirt, where the Crypt Keeper leered up at me. Mom hated this shirt. Well, she hated all my horror shirts. But this one especially. "No, I've only seen the show. Are the comics good?"

She swung her legs off the table, combat boots clunking on the floor. "Good? They're *classic*. They—"

"Hang on, Mi Jin," Jess interrupted. "Meeting, remember? We need to get started."

"Sorry," Mi Jin said cheerfully. "We'll talk *Crypt* later, Kat."

"Okay!"

I closed the door quietly. Everyone seemed nice enough, and not nearly as weird as I'd worried they might be. Well, Roland was kind of annoying. *Hormone central.* Right. Now, if Grandma had been there in the same room as Sam Sumners, *that* would've been hormone central.

All the same, I couldn't deny that I was curious about Oscar.

When I got to the top of the stairs and saw the laptop Lidia mentioned, my thoughts turned to something far more important than Oscar—the Internet. I sat down eagerly, but paused with my hand over the mouse.

The PRINT window was open, and the arrow hovered over "Yes," as if someone had left in the middle of a printing job. I stared at the screen, thinking. The crew probably used this laptop for work, and I didn't want to accidentally mess something up.

Still . . . I hadn't been online in, like, twelve hours.

I grabbed the mouse. Whoever had left this open clearly wanted to print it. I'd just do it for them.

A green light flashed on the little portable printer next to the laptop, and the first sheet began sliding through. On the screen, the print window vanished. The word processor was still open, but to a blank page.

"Weird." Shrugging, I closed it, then opened a browser and logged into my e-mail account.

From: trishhhhbequiet@mymail.net
To: acciopancakes@mymail.net
Subject: COME BAAAAAACK!!!!

seriously, it's only been a day, and life is intolerable without you. what's rotterdam like? is the cast nice? is sam really ditzy? mark wants to know if they'll let you be on the show. (would they?? it'd be so crazy to see you on TV!) your blog looks awesome—can't wait for the first ghost story!
can we video chat soon? it's weird not having you here. :(
<3 trish

Reading Trish's e-mail was strange—it made me smile, but my throat got kind of tight. I pulled up my blog and scrolled down to find three comments on my first post. But before I could read the first one, a muffled *click* made me jump.

I looked around. The door to the projection room was closed, and I was fairly sure it had been open when I got upstairs. I'd almost forgotten about Oscar. Standing, I'd taken only a step when the paper sticking out of the printer caught my eye.

It wasn't blank.

Glancing at the door to the projection room again, I grabbed the page.

KEEP HER AWAY FROM THE MEDIUM

"Oookay." I glanced around but didn't see a trash can. Folding the page a few times, I stuck it in my jeans pocket and opened the door to the projection room.

Boxes and old pieces of equipment cluttered the floor. Straight ahead, I saw the small window overlooking the auditorium, and in front of it, the projector. And next to the projector . . . a boy.

His back was to me, head bowed, shoulders hunched.

"Oscar?"

He didn't move. Slowly, I took a step forward, then another. Was he crying?

"Hello?" I tried again, louder this time. Nothing. When I was within arm's reach, I touched his shoulder lightly. "Are you okay?"

At last, he turned around. And I found myself staring into black, empty sockets.

CHAPTER FOUR

IT CAME FROM THE LASER PRINTER

Post: Travel Is a Beating
Comments: (3)
trishhhh: miss u! seen anything spooky yet?
MARK: ghost pics?
EdieM: Sam pics?

HE had massive yellow fangs, too. And blood smeared around his mouth.

"You've got something on your chin," I informed him, keeping my voice as flat as possible. Reaching up, he pulled the mask off—brown eyes, black hair, normal teeth, blood-free mouth—and glared at me.

"Geez, you didn't even scream."

I shrugged. "Why would I scream at something so obviously fake?"

"It worked on Mi Jin," he said defensively. "She screamed so loud, Jess said you could hear her out on the street."

"Well, either she was faking it or she scares insanely easy," I retorted. "I'm Kat, by the way."

"I figured. Nice to meet you." His voice indicated it wasn't nice at all. "I'm Oscar."

"I figured."

We didn't shake hands.

"Okay, then," I said after a few seconds. "I'm going to use the laptop for a while. Unless you need it?"

"Nope."

"Okay." I left the projection room without another word.

Sitting back down behind the laptop, I pulled up the comments on my blog post, smiling as I read. If Grandma thought I'd be taking stealth photos of Sam's butt, she was dead wrong. Just before I clicked REPLY to tell her so, Oscar appeared at my side. He leaned against the table, setting the gruesome mask next to the mouse.

"So how long do you think your dad'll last?"

I stared at him. "Excuse me?"

"You know, hosting," Oscar said. "He's the fourth host. The job's cursed."

I snorted. "Right, I forgot about that."

The most haunted show on television was, of course, "cursed." The curse was that they couldn't keep a host. Because it couldn't just be that the low budget and lower ratings drove people to quit. Nope, must be evil spirits.

"You should check out the *P2P* forums," Oscar told me. "They're all taking bets. Most of them think he'll be gone after two episodes."

"Whatever." I turned back to the screen, taking care to sound as indifferent as possible. But his words nagged at me. It was weird to think that a bunch of fans online were gossiping about my dad.

Oscar leaned forward, squinting. *"The Kat Sinclair Files?"*

29

"My blog," I said, resisting the urge to close the laptop so he couldn't see. "Mostly just to keep in touch with my grandma and my friends Trish and Mark." Oscar's hand twitched, and his expression went from surprised to oddly closed in a heartbeat. I stared at him curiously. "Something wrong?"

"No," he said flatly. "I had a friend named Mark, too, that's all."

"Oh." I clicked REPLY, wishing he'd go away. "Had? What, is he dead or something?" After a few seconds of typing, I looked up to find Oscar staring at me.

"Oh God, your friend didn't actually die, did he?" I said nervously. "I was just kidding, I didn't—"

Oscar rolled his eyes. "Quit freaking out. He's not dead."

"Oh." I waited, because it looked like he was going to say something else. But he just stood there. I turned back to my screen just as the door swung open.

"Hey, guys!" Mi Jin stepped inside. "Meeting's almost over—Jess is still going over some stuff with your dad, though."

"Okay," I said. "So you got stuck teaching us, huh?"

Mi Jin laughed. "I guess. It'll be fun, though. Your dad and Lidia told me you guys both have pretty good grades."

"I tried this out on Kat," Oscar informed her, twirling the mask around his finger. "Your reaction was way better."

"Yeah, I'll be starring in a slasher movie one day, just you wait," Mi Jin said with a grin. "My mom used to say my scream could shatter glass." She nodded at the door. "We just ordered some lunch if you guys are hungry."

My stomach rumbled again. "Starving," I said, closing my window on the laptop. Then I remembered the page I'd printed. "Should I leave this on? I think someone was using it before I came in."

Mi Jin shook her head. "Nah, we've all been downstairs all morning. You and Oscar are the only ones who've been up here."

"But there was a . . ." I trailed off, glancing at Oscar. He stared back, his expression blank. "Never mind."

I followed them out of the room, watching Oscar twirl that stupid mask around his finger and thinking of the message folded up in my pocket. *KEEP HER AWAY FROM THE MEDIUM.* Another prank, no doubt. He'd probably typed it up right before I got upstairs, then hid to watch my reaction. Apparently he was into playing jokes on people. Very unfunny ones, too.

And I was stuck with him as a classmate. Awesome.

After lunch (sandwiches with cold cuts and probably the best cheese I'd ever tasted), I slammed into a wall of exhaustion. Oscar had spent the whole meal having an intense debate with Mi Jin about some video game. Jess was going over the Crimptown story in detail with Dad and Lidia. It actually sounded really interesting, but my eyelids drooped like my lashes were weights. When my head slipped off my hand and I jerked awake, Oscar snickered.

"I need some air," I announced in the most dignified voice I could muster, righting the jar of pickles I'd knocked over before heading for the door.

Roland was outside of the theater, sitting on a backpack

with a sucker sticking out of his mouth. I sped up, hoping he wouldn't want to talk.

"So, Kat," Roland said. Groaning inwardly, I stopped and turned to face him. Time for some awkward conversation. Dislike. "Parents just split up, huh?"

I blinked, startled. "Uh . . . yeah. My dad told you?"

Roland lifted a shoulder. "He mentioned it. But it wouldn't have been hard to guess."

Before I could respond—and I had no idea what to say to that, anyway—Sam Sumners wandered around the corner of the theater. His eyes looked glazed over, like he was half-asleep. I could empathize.

"It was her brother," he said to no one in particular. Roland pulled the sucker out of his mouth and shot Sam a purplish grin.

"Her brother? Really? You usually say it's a boyfriend or husband. These things are always about jealousy."

Sam nodded vaguely. "Usually, yes . . . but not this time."

I cleared my throat. "What are you guys talking about?"

Turning, Sam squinted at me with a strange expression, as if he wasn't quite sure whether I was real. I had the sudden crazy idea that he could see ghosts better than living people. "Sonja Hillebrandt," Sam said. "Her presence is quieter than the pirate's, but more rooted to this place. The pirate wants to roam."

"Um . . ." I glanced at Roland for help.

"Sonja's one of the Crimptown ghosts," he explained, crunching down on the purple sucker with a sharp *crack*. "Sam's trying to figure out why she's still hanging around.

Apparently, it has something to do with her brother."

Sam frowned, his eyes glazing over once more. "Protective . . . she's very protective . . ."

I stared as he wandered off around the corner of the theater without another word. "He looks like he needs some sleep."

"He's fine," Roland replied. "That's just how he acts when we're on-site. It's an occupational hazard when you're a medium. Hard to communicate with the dead and not walk around looking like a zombie."

Crossing my arms, I studied Roland. He sounded mocking, although I wasn't sure if it was me or Sam he was making fun of. "You're a parapsychologist, right? Like a *paranormal* psychologist?"

"Parapsychologist, like a scientist who looks for evidence of any sort of paranormal activity, such as clairvoyance, precognition, and telepathy." Roland yawned widely. "Or, you know. A spook shrink, if you prefer."

Was he making fun of himself now? This guy was so weird.

"Okay, I have to ask," I said. "Do you really believe in all this?"

"All what?"

"You know, *this.*" I gestured to the theater. "Ghosts, haunted tunnels, a walking Ken doll who thinks he can talk to dead people."

Roland let out a snort of laughter. "Walking Ken doll. Nice."

I winced. "Sorry, it's a joke I have with my grandmother.

She's got the hots for him pretty bad."

What? Seriously, brain. Time to start controlling the words coming out of my mouth.

Roland was still chuckling. "Oh no, your grandma's a Sumner Stalker?"

"A *what*?"

"That's what Sam's 'fans' call themselves." He made little air quotation marks with his fingers on the word *fans*. "They get pretty intense."

I made a face. "She's not that bad, I promise."

"Glad to hear it," Roland said around his sucker. "You should see some of his fan mail—it gets pretty creepy. And he never realizes when they cross the line. He's way more tuned in with the dead than with the living. Pretty sure that's why he gets those kinds of fans, actually."

"What do you mean?" I asked curiously. "He's got fans because he's . . . well, good-looking."

Roland shrugged. "True, but he's also haunted. You don't make a career out of contacting the dead without a reason. And people are drawn to that."

I frowned. He had a point. I knew Sam's story from all the interviews Grandma showed me—how he'd fallen into the deep end of a pool when he was little and it was a few minutes before someone found him and gave him CPR. He'd nearly drowned, and ever since then, he claimed to have a connection with the spirit world.

But Sam wasn't the only one who was haunted by something. Everyone on *Passport to Paranormal* had, for one reason or another, decided to chase ghosts for a living. Maybe everyone had a Thing that haunted them, that they wanted to escape.

"Our first host was a Sumner Stalker," Roland was saying, his expression sour. "Emily Rosinski. Total nutjob. Wasn't sorry to see her go."

"What about the other two?" I asked, thinking of the so-called curse. "The hosts?"

"Carlos was fired. Bernice just got freaked out and quit."

"So you don't believe in the host curse, then?" I asked. "Or any of this 'most haunted show' stuff?"

Roland shrugged. "It doesn't matter what I believe. That's not what the show is about."

"Really? I kind of thought that was the whole point of your job," I said. "Finding proof of paranormal activity."

His eyebrows shot up. "Proof? Like what—video of a ghost? A photo? You seem like a smart kid. What do you think would happen if we put that on the air?"

I thought about it. "I guess people would say you faked it."

"Exactly." Roland tossed the sucker stick into a trash can. "It's a no-win situation." He pulled another sucker out of his pocket.

"What's with all the suckers?" I asked, watching as he ripped off the wrapper. This one was red.

"We just had lunch," Roland said matter-of-factly. "Normally I'd be having a cigarette right now, but I quit. Therefore..." He waved the sucker at me before sticking it in his mouth. "I've got more. Want one?"

"No, thanks," I said. "So what did you mean, it's a no-win situation?"

Roland leaned back against the wall and closed his eyes. "If we prove ghosts exist—people think it's fake. If we find nothing—people think it's boring."

"Well, you find *some* creepy stuff sometimes," I said thoughtfully. "I mean, I don't think everyone who watches the show believes in ghosts, or wants proof or whatever. I think most of them just like being scared. They want something to talk about."

"Dead on," Roland agreed. "That's why we do our best to make things . . . entertaining."

"What do you mean?"

The door opened again, and Lidia stuck her head out. "We need you guys in about five minutes," she said, then looked around. "Isn't Sam out here?"

"Wandered off," Roland said. "I'll find him." Once Lidia was gone, he stood up, shouldering his backpack. "So what about you?"

"Huh?"

Roland looked at me expectantly. "Do you believe in ghosts?"

"Nope," I replied firmly.

The corners of his mouth twitched up a little. "Good. You'll have more fun that way."

I stared after him as he sauntered around the corner where Sam had vanished. Slipping my fingers in my pocket, I pulled out the piece of paper again. *KEEP HER AWAY FROM THE MEDIUM.* I frowned. I'd clicked print, but the document had been blank on the screen. Even if this was just another one of Oscar's pranks, how could he have managed that? It was more like a computer glitch ... but then again, *someone* had typed this message. This warning about a medium.

Was it about Sam? And who was supposed to stay away from him?

After a second, I rolled my eyes. It hadn't even been a day and I was already getting creeped out over nothing.

Shoving the paper in my pocket, I headed back into the theater.

Post: The Pirate Ghost of Crimptown

I don't believe in ghosts. (Sorry, Grandma.)

I just figured that since this is my first real, not-jet-lagged blog post, I should make that clear before I say anything else about *P2P*. I don't believe in ghosts—but I do love scary stories.

For the first episode, we're spending the night in Crimptown, which is this supposedly haunted system of tunnels under Rotterdam. This morning, I watched Dad interview a guy who owns a restaurant on the waterfront that's been around since the 1800s. He told Dad all about the legend of Crimptown and why people think it's haunted.

A bunch of the bars and hotels and restaurants in downtown Rotterdam have cellars connected by the tunnels. The tunnels all lead to the waterfront, because the point was to easily get food and supplies from the boats to the businesses. There were pulley systems to get the supplies up to street level, and chutes to drop stuff down into the cellars for storage.

Sometime in the mid-1800s, a bunch of men in Rotterdam started going missing. And they were always last seen at a bar. After a while, people noticed another connection—all the bars they disappeared from were connected to the Crimptown tunnel system.

It turned out a pirate named Falk Von Leer had this horrible scheme going on. He'd get someone at the bar to drug the guy's drink. After the guy passed out, they'd throw him down one of the chutes into the cellar. From there, Red Leer would have his crew members drag the guy through the tunnels to the waterfront, and then he would sell his prisoner into slavery on cargo ships. (His nickname in Dutch is Rood Leer—*rood* means *red* in English. The restaurant owner said they called him that because of all the blood he spilled.)

Everyone knew what Red Leer was doing, but they were all too afraid to do something about it. But when a teenage boy named Bastian Hillebrandt went missing, his older sister Sonja decided to organize a rescue. She gathered a group of women whose husbands or sons or brothers had all been kidnapped by Red Leer. One night, the women disguised themselves as men, secretly armed themselves with all kinds of weapons, and visited all the bars connected to the tunnels. They ordered drinks but didn't actually drink them, and pretended to pass out like they'd been drugged. Once they got thrown down the trapdoors into the cellars, they attacked Red Leer's men and freed all the prisoners who hadn't been sold to ships yet. Sonja came face-to-face with Red Leer and demanded he return her brother. Red Leer refused and then he killed her. But the freed prisoners and all the women who had joined Sonja attacked and killed Red Leer. Eventually, all the men Red Leer had kidnapped and sold were found and set free.

But both Red Leer's and Sonja's ghosts are said to haunt Crimptown, forever at war with each other.

The guy Dad interviewed said people who tour Crimptown report all sorts of strange stuff, like flickering lights or chilly breezes. Sam says he can "feel the tension between Sonja and Red Leer in my gut." Roland says Sam just ate some bad oysters. (Honestly, I can't even tell if Roland believes in any of this stuff. He's weird like that.)

As for me, I'm still feeling pretty skeptical. Wouldn't ALL old tunnel systems have bad lighting and chilly breezes? I mean, it would take a lot more than that for me to consider a place haunted. But I guess I'll find out tonight, since we'll be camping out down there. Either way, it's a really cool story. And I found these portraits of Sonja and Red Leer online. Isn't Red Leer creepy-looking?

WHEN Grandma had first suggested the blog, I'd thought it sounded like too much work. But it turns out when you don't have to worry about outlines and a thesis statement and grades and all that stuff, writing is pretty fun. After watching Dad's interview, I'd wandered along the waterfront until I found an Internet café where I could write up Sonja and Red Leer's story and add their portraits. Red Leer had a thick, curled mustache and a ghoulish grin. Sonja looked so . . . innocent. And normal. Just a kind-faced woman with dark hair wearing a simple dress and a delicate smile. It was hard to imagine her leading an attack on a band of pirates.

Once I published my post, I found the *Passport to Paranormal* forums. I couldn't help it—I had to see what people were saying about my dad. The top thread had his name in the title. I scanned the first page quickly.

P2P FAN FORUMS
Meet Jack Sinclair, Victim #4

Maytrix [admin]
Okay, guys, we've got ourselves another host! But for how long? *evil laugh*
So, Jack Sinclair hosted a morning show in Chelsea, Ohio, for several years. You can watch clips of him <u>here</u> . . . seems like a fun guy. Let's recap our former *P2P* hosts:
Victim #1: Emily Rosinski, sixteen episodes
Victim #2: Carlos Ortiz, eight episodes
Victim #3: Bernice Boyd, four episodes
On to Victim #4! Thoughts?

spicychai [member]
two episodes. do the math.

YourCohortInCrime [member]
IDK, this "host curse" thing they're doing can't really last, right?
It's obviously just for publicity—the ratings shoot up for a few
episodes every time. Remember when Carlos published that
exposé? He said they fake all kinds of stuff on the show. That's
why he got fired. And the first episode with Bernice as host after
Carlos left had the highest ratings they'd ever seen.

beautifulgollum [moderator]
Firing hosts isn't good publicity, YCIC. And Carlos denied writing
that exposé—he said he was set up. The curse is because the
show is haunted—some restless spirit has been with them since
the first episode in the lighthouse. I think that spirit is responsible
for getting rid of the other hosts. Hopefully it will approve of Jack.

AntiSimon [member]
I miss Bernice. (Anyone's better than Emily, though.) Anyway, I
think spicychai's right—the length of time is cut in half from one
host to the next, so Jack's got two episodes. My prediction: Jack
does a couple of episodes and then they go hostless. Let Samland
take over the whole thing. (Or the show gets canceled . . . and
let's face it, that's a pretty big possibility.)
   BTW, the fact that the timing works like that PROVES the curse
is real. It can't be a coincidence.

YourCohortInCrime [member]
Uh, wrong. It proves the producer firing the hosts for publicity can
do basic math like the rest of us.

beautifulgollum [moderator]
Come on, YCIC—the point of the show is to find ghosts. They
don't WANT to lose hosts.

YourCohortInCrime [member]
Funny, I could've sworn the point of the show was ratings.

Thomas Cooper's gonna can it if it doesn't do better this season.

I got to the bottom of the page and clicked over to the next . . . and then the next. It was kind of unnerving, watching all these fans make bets on my dad and bicker about whether his job was cursed.

Did they really believe a *ghost* was getting rid of the hosts? I mean, weren't these people supposed to be adults? Even more interesting was that some of them seemed to think Lidia was actually firing hosts just to make viewers *think* there was a curse, like a publicity stunt.

The weirdest thing was that no one knew where the old hosts all went. Not like any of them were all that famous, but Emily Rosinski and Carlos Ortiz were reporters before joining the show, and Bernice Boyd had worked for the History channel. And apparently they were all way low-profile now, refusing to give interviews or talk to anyone about why they left. That was a big part of why the ratings always went up—all the mystery and drama surrounding their sudden departures.

Fans loved gossiping about Emily, in particular—and they didn't say very nice things. I remembered the face Roland made when he called her a "Sumner Stalker." A lot of fans thought she'd quit because Sam didn't return her feelings, but some speculated they secretly dated and had a huge breakup. Personally, I couldn't imagine Sam dating anyone. (Well, anyone *living*. He'd probably date a ghost if he could.)

There were tons of other interesting threads, too. The forums were organized by season and episode, but also by topic. The most popular thread was about Sam and Roland—or "Samland," which made me snort my soda. I wondered if Roland knew about that particular nickname.

As much as I wanted to just sit in that cushy chair and bask in an Internet glow all day, I didn't think Dad would appreciate me blowing twenty euros here when he had a laptop (no matter how clunky and slow it was). So when my hour was up, I logged off and headed back to the hotel. I found Dad in our room, studying his laptop screen.

"Hi, Dad."

"Hey, sweetie," he said distractedly.

I flopped back on my bed. "What's that?"

"Just reading up on the local history." He smiled, eyes still on the screen. "Crimptown is fascinating, isn't it?"

"Yeah." I yawned widely. "Hey, Dad?"

"Mmhmm?"

I paused, trying to think of how to ask the question. *Why'd you choose this job?* But that would only lead to more questions I wasn't sure I wanted answered. *Why do you want to chase ghosts? What if Mom decides to come back?*

Did she leave because of the Thing?

"Kat?"

I glanced over to find him staring at me in concern.

"Um . . . can I use the laptop when you're done?"

"Of course."

He turned back to the screen and started pecking away at the keyboard. Within a minute, I was sound asleep.

CHAPTER SIX
WHAT LURKS IN THE
CYBERSHADOWS

From: acciopancakes@mymail.net
To: EdieM@mymail.net
Subject: This whole curse thing

Hi, Grandma,
I found the *P2P* forums (those people are kind of insane btw).
What did you think of the other hosts? Roland said Emily Rosinski
was a nutjob because she had a huge crush on Sam. Do you think
maybe they've been firing the hosts just so fans will think the
show is cursed? I don't want that to happen to Dad. Pretty sure
he's not ready to go home yet.
Love, Kat

"YOU know what?"

Mi Jin and I both glanced up. Oscar was sprawled
out on an old sofa, lazily kicking the door to the theater's
projection room in a steady rhythm. *Thud. Thud. Thud.*

"What?" Mi Jin swiveled away from the laptop, one hand
still on the keyboard.

Oscar tapped his math sheet with his pencil. "There are
fifty-three questions on this."

"And?"

"And I think that's *irrational.*"

Mi Jin laughed. I rolled my eyes, focusing on my own sheet. I'd slept a record-setting eleven hours straight last night, but it still didn't feel like enough. When I'd woken up at seven this morning—with *no* alarm, which was pretty freaky—I felt great. But the closer we got to lunchtime, the more I wanted to crawl back into bed.

A few minutes passed, during which I tried to ignore the fact that my eyelids were beginning to droop. Suddenly, Oscar dropped his pencil on the floor next to me.

"Done." He leaned over, and I shifted in my spot so he couldn't see my work and stared resolutely at the page.

1.92 – 5.6
A) integer
B) rational
C) irrational

"You're not done yet?"

I pressed my lips together. "No."

Oscar sighed wearily. "Are you at least close?"

I ignored him, and after a few seconds, he leaned back on the sofa.

Thud. Thud. Thud.

"Could you maybe quit that?" I asked through gritted teeth.

"Quit what?"

Thud. Thud. Thud.

"*That,*" I said sharply, flipping my page over. "And by the way, fifty-three is a rational number."

Oscar groaned. "I know. It was a *joke*. Man, you have no sense of humor."

"I do, actually." I punched a few keys on my calculator. "I laugh when something's funny."

Thud. Thud. Thud.

"Oscar, I swear to—"

"*Okay*," Mi Jin cut in loudly. "It's almost time for lunch—Oscar, will you go see if Lidia's ordered anything yet?"

"Sure." Swinging his legs off the sofa, Oscar stood and stretched. "Let me know if you need help with that," he said, then sauntered out of the room before I could think of a response.

I stared after him in disbelief, then realized Mi Jin was giggling. "Sorry," she said quickly. "You two really push each other's buttons, huh?"

"He's just. So. *Obnoxious*." I set my pencil on the floor next to me and rubbed my eyes. "I mean, seriously. I've never met anyone so annoying, it's like he—"

"Kat," Mi Jin interrupted. I lowered my hands to find Lidia in the doorway, and my face went hot.

"Oh . . . hi."

Smiling, Lidia walked over to the desk and started rifling through a folder. "Talking about my nephew?"

"Well . . ." I hesitated. "Yeah. Sorry."

She laughed. "It's okay. Although I promise he's usually a nice kid. He's just had a rough time this year."

"He said he got expelled for fighting?" Mi Jin asked, and I glanced up.

Lidia nodded. "Yeah. Poor thing . . . lots of bullying at his school."

I snorted quietly, hiding my face behind my worksheet. It was pretty much impossible to imagine someone as arrogant as Oscar getting bullied. He seemed more likely to be a bully himself.

"Kat, do you need any help with that?" Mi Jin asked, pulling her hair back into a ponytail and pointing at my worksheet with her boot.

"Nah, thanks. I've only got four problems left."

"Just leave it in the folder when you're done, okay?"

"Okay."

I stared at the same problem, the numbers swimming in front of my eyes. I was so taking a nap after lunch. My head felt like it was stuffed with tissue, and a muffled beeping sound filled my ears. It was a few seconds before I realized it was coming from Lidia.

"Sorry," she said, pulling her phone out of her pocket and silencing the alarm. "Just a reminder to take my pills." Setting the folder down, she unzipped a small purple bag next to the laptop and took out a bottle.

"Are you sick?" I asked, watching as she shook a few pills into her hand.

Taking a swig of water, Lidia popped the pills and swallowed. "A minor heart problem. Nothing serious."

My eyes widened in surprise. "*Heart* problems? Aren't you a little young for that?" I winced as soon as the words were out of my mouth, but Lidia just smiled.

"It's a condition I was born with," she explained, setting her water bottle down. "Seizures, fainting, the works. I had a pacemaker put in when I was eight."

"Oh." I watched Lidia toy with the locket on her necklace. "I'm sorry."

"Oh, it's fine," Lidia said. "Kind of a bummer when I was younger, though. Strobe lights can trigger my seizures, so that meant no concerts or haunted houses. Not that that stopped me," she added with a wink. I grinned as she tucked the pill bottle back inside the purple bag. "Are you coming down for lunch?"

"Um . . ." My eyes strayed to the laptop, where the Internet beckoned. Lidia laughed, heading to the door.

"I'll make sure to save you some food. Take your time."

"Thanks."

Flopping down onto the desk chair, I logged into my e-mail account. As much as I was trying not to let it bother me, I couldn't help thinking about the host curse. To my relief, Grandma had already responded to the e-mail I'd sent her before breakfast.

From: EdieM@mymail.net
To: acciopancakes@mymail.net
Re: This whole curse thing

Hi, KitKat,
So now you're lurking in the *P2P* forums, hmm? I suppose I'll have to watch what I say in there from now on.

I groaned. So Grandma was one of the fans in the forum. What a surprise. I wondered what her screen name was, then immediately decided I didn't want to know. Ever. *Ever.*

I agree, it's pretty weird to watch them all argue about my son-in-law. Try not to take what you read on the boards too seriously. Lidia isn't just firing hosts for publicity. This is a show that struggles with low ratings—people are going to come and go, that's just how it is. And it's true that ratings go up when a host leaves, but that lasts only an episode or two. Not exactly a smart long-term publicity plan, right?

The other hosts . . . Bernice was really knowledgeable about the local history and folklore, but she was skittish—afraid of her own shadow. Why she ever took the job is beyond me. Carlos did indeed publish a piece accusing the crew of faking things, and he was promptly canned—although he always said he didn't actually write it. And Emily couldn't have cared less about ghosts. She spent every episode doing nothing but fawning all over Sam. I guess after a while he must have rejected her, and she flounced. (And good riddance! She was a poor representative of us Sumner Stalkers.) Funny that you talked to Roland about that. It was always obvious that the way Emily acted around Sam bothered him. Between you and me, I think he was a bit jealous.

I smiled, but something nagged at me. *Sumner Stalkers.* I knew Grandma probably thought that name was funny, but I couldn't help remembering what Roland had said. *Our first host was a Sumner Stalker. Total nutjob.*

Would he consider Grandma a nutjob, too? She really wasn't. No one knew the difference between a fan and a real stalker better than Grandma. She got threatening letters for almost two years after *Mutant Cheerleaders Attack* came out, before the police finally caught the guy. That was way before I was born, but she'd told me all about it. It sounded really scary.

I wondered, too, if Grandma was right about Roland

being jealous. He definitely looked irritated when he talked about Emily. If he'd been in love with her and had to watch her flirt with Sam all the time, well, I guess that would be pretty annoying.

Yawning, I opened a chat window and checked for Trish and Mark—both gray, both off-line. Which made sense, seeing as it was, like, six in the morning there. A wave of homesickness hit, and I had the sudden urge to call one of them, or Grandma, or . . .

One of my contacts abruptly flipped from gray to green, and my heart leaped. Then I saw the name.

MonicaMills [Mom]

I froze, my hand on the mouse. And sure enough, after a few seconds:

Kat? Are you there?

A lump rose in my throat. Numbly, I clicked the chat window closed and logged out. Then I shoved my unfinished math worksheet in Mi Jin's folder and went to go get some lunch.

CHAPTER SEVEN
IF LOOKS COULD KILL

MonicaMills [Mom]
This contact has been blocked. To unblock, go to your privacy settings.

MY after-lunch nap turned out to be a total bust. I lay on my bed staring at the ugly hotel curtains for almost forty-five minutes before giving up and heading to the waterfront to join the crew.

After stopping to buy a soda, I peered up and down the boardwalk until I spotted them huddled together. A cool breeze ruffled my hair as I walked, and I shivered—I still hadn't gotten used to my short cut. The back of my neck felt weirdly exposed.

Still, the crisp air woke me up from my post-almost-nap trance. And I wasn't the only one out enjoying the perfect fall weather. I squinted down at the crew, wondering if the crowds of families and couples strolling along the boardwalk were making it difficult to get the shots they needed.

Ring, ring! Glancing over my shoulder, I jumped out of the way just as a cyclist went zipping past. When I turned back around, I slammed into someone and dropped my soda bottle.

"Oh, *great.*" Kneeling down, the dark-haired woman scooped her binoculars and camera up and away from a trickle of soda. I winced, picking up the bottle.

"Sorry, I didn't . . ." Pausing, I tried frantically to remember how to say sorry in Dutch. Then I realized she'd spoken English. It was hard to tell thanks to her oversize sunglasses, but I was pretty sure she was looking at me like I'd just kicked a kitten.

"Just look where you're going, kid," she snapped in a high, nasal voice, tucking a strand of hair behind her ear. She was young, and her face was really angular—she looked almost gaunt.

"Sorry," I said again, not bothering to hide my irritation as she made a show of inspecting her camera. "Is it broken?"

Rather than answering, she just turned and headed in the opposite direction, muttering under her breath. Rolling my eyes, I tossed my empty soda bottle in the trash and headed toward the crew.

I couldn't help picturing the Elapse E-250 still stuffed in my suitcase. With so many interesting sights around—the boats, the vendors, little kids playing jump rope—the urge to take photographs was strong. Unfortunately, that urge always came with my mom's voice giving instructions.

Look, that girl over there near the railing; such a textured background with the boats behind her . . . The light is dim this time of day, so use a slower shutter speed . . .

Keeping my eyes firmly fixed on the crew, I walked fast and avoided looking for any more frame-worthy moments. Dad and Lidia were side by side going over Dad's notes, while Jess adjusted the large video camera on her shoulder. Sam was watching a group of teenagers take photos near the water. Roland simply looked bored. I noticed Oscar hovering around Mi Jin and stifled a groan—I'd been hoping he stayed back at the hotel.

"Almost ready, guys," Jess said. "Mi Jin, Jack's going to need the windscreen."

"Got it!" Mi Jin rummaged through the massive camera bag hanging off her shoulder. A second later, she let out a bloodcurdling scream and flung something long and wriggly straight at me.

I jumped back as a snake went sailing past my head. It hit the boardwalk with a *smack* and . . . laid there. I took a hesitant step forward, then nudged it with my toe.

"Fake," I said, giving Oscar a pointed look. "Totally fake."

"Oscar, come on," Lidia groaned, but the others started laughing. No one laughed harder than Mi Jin, though. Which was kind of disappointing. It would've been fun to watch her chew him out.

But she seemed to find the whole thing hilarious. "Nice one," she told Oscar, still snickering as she handed Dad a cover for his mic. "That's two to one, then?"

"Yours didn't count," Oscar said with a grin. "I'm not afraid of spiders."

"You jumped a little." Mi Jin zipped the camera bag closed. "But yeah, your reaction was nowhere near as epic as mine."

"You scared off some of this crowd." Roland sounded mildly appreciative as he glanced around the boardwalk.

"That was a pretty legit scream."

Mi Jin beamed. "Horror movie–worthy, right?"

"I'll say."

I smiled at Dad and he winked. Grandma would love Mi Jin.

"All right, we need to get this wrapped up in the next hour," Jess announced, shifting under the weight of the camera. "Jack, we'll shoot the first thirty seconds in place, then get the three of you walking toward the theater. Let's get a couple of takes of the intro first, all right?"

Dad nodded, handing Lidia his notes. "Sounds good."

I took several steps back as everyone else got into their places, and something squished under my foot. Stooping down, I picked up the rubber snake just as Oscar reached my side.

"Not afraid of snakes either, huh?" he asked.

"Not fake ones."

"Real ones, though?"

"Not really," I said, watching as Dad launched into a description of life in Rotterdam in the eighteen hundreds. "Trish has a pet snake. His name's Fang, but he's harmless." I glanced at Oscar. "I mean, if you'd hidden a live cobra in there or something, I might have screamed."

To my surprise, he cracked a smile. "*Might* have?"

I shrugged. "Yeah. And I *might* have jumped over that railing and swum to England."

Oscar actually laughed a little. Before either of us could say anything else, Jess let out a frustrated cry.

"*Cut.* Sorry, Jack . . . what is *wrong* with this thing?"

Mi Jin joined Jess and Lidia in inspecting the camera. "What *is* this? An error code?" Jess asked Mi Jin, who frowned.

"I've never seen that come up before . . ." After a second, Mi Jin whirled around to face Oscar, her eyes wide. "Is this another prank? Did you do this?" she asked. Confusion flickered across Oscar's face.

"Do what?"

Jess was shaking her head. "No way, he couldn't have."

She turned slightly so we could see the viewfinder. The screen was black, but a row of letters scrolled rapidly at the bottom.

XXXXXXXXXXXX . . . XXXXXXXXXXXX . . . XXXXXXXXXXXX . . .

Dad frowned, leaning closer. "Maybe try turning it off?"

Jess obliged, pressing the button. But the scrolling continued.

"Thirteen *X*s," Mi Jin said excitedly. "Ah, what am I doing—we need to get a picture of this! Anyone have a camera? Wait, there's a handheld in here somewhere . . ."

My fingers twitched at my side as Mi Jin dug the small camera out of her bag, my thoughts once again drifting to the Elapse. I watched Mi Jin begin filming the scrolling letters on the viewfinder. Sam drifted over to stand next to Jess.

"Thirteen *X*s," he mused. "A message from the beyond."

Roland looked highly amused. "Must be."

"Wait . . . I feel something." Sam's expression was so intense I had to bite the inside of my cheek to keep from laughing. "There is a presence with us."

Mi Jin stepped back, grinning, as Roland joined Sam in the shot. "Is it Red Leer?" he asked Sam in a low, serious voice. "Tell him we're not scheduled to be drugged and kidnapped until tomorrow night."

Oscar and I started to snicker as Sam squinted and looked around like he was trying to locate a ghost pirate standing among the rest of us. His gaze rested on me, and my laughter faded. "I'm not sure it's Red Leer," he mused, apparently oblivious to Roland's sarcasm. "I'm not sensing a lot of anger."

"Ah. Should I antagonize him, then?" Roland cleared his throat loudly, but Jess cut him off.

"Look, it's stopped." She turned slightly so we could see the viewfinder, which was back to normal. Jess swung around, aiming the camera at Dad. "Ready to give the intro another shot?"

Dad gave her the thumbs-up. Sam glanced at me again before turning away, and I felt slightly unsettled.

As they started filming, Mi Jin hung back and zipped the camera up in her bag. She glanced over at Oscar and me. "How'd you do it, though, seriously?" she asked in a low, eager voice.

Oscar's brow furrowed. "Do what?"

"Thirteen *X*s!" Mi Jin said. "You did it, right? Like what you did to Lidia's EMF meter yesterday? But how—"

"What did you do to her EMF?" I interrupted, picturing the gadget Lidia had pulled out of her purse yesterday when she was searching for granola bars.

Oscar shrugged. "Messed with the calibration a little so that it went nuts when we first got to the theater."

"But how'd you get those *X*s on the camera?" Mi Jin pressed, and Oscar grinned.

"It's a secret."

Mi Jin laughed. "Well, good one," she said with a wink, then hurried back over to the others.

I stared at Oscar. If he knew enough about electronics to sabotage Lidia's EMF, maybe he really had somehow gotten that message to print out. "Did you type up that thing about the medium?" I blurted out.

Oscar blinked. "The *what*?"

"The message," I said impatiently. "The one that printed out yesterday when you were hiding in the projection room with that stupid mask. *Keep her away from the medium.* You did it, right?"

"Hang on there, crazy," Oscar retorted. "I have no clue what you're talking about."

I scowled. "So you messed with Lidia's EMF and Jess's camera, but *not* with the laptop up in the projection room?"

He opened his mouth but hesitated, glancing back at the camera. I crossed my arms impatiently. He really didn't seem to know anything about the medium message. And I was positive he looked confused when Mi Jin first suggested he'd tampered with the camera. Maybe he really had nothing to do with either. Maybe they were both just glitches.

Or maybe Oscar was an amazingly good liar.

Oscar was still staring at the camera. Jess handed it over to Mi Jin, then joined Lidia and the others to go over the next take. Mi Jin turned away from them, studying the viewfinder closely. Then she glanced over at Oscar and me.

"Just tell me how you did it!" she called. "Please?"

Oscar looked pleased. "Didn't you say you majored in electrical engineering? You figure it out!"

Laughing, Mi Jin turned her attention back to the viewfinder. "Touché."

I stared at Oscar for a second, then grinned. "*Oh*. I get it."

"Get what?"

"Why you lied about the camera," I said lightly. "You didn't do it, but you want Mi Jin to *think* you did. I know she's impressed and all, but she's a little old for you, don't you think?"

I waited for a defensive comeback, a blush, anything. For a few seconds, Oscar just gazed at me. Then he started cracking up.

"You're right," he said. "You're totally right. I don't have a chance." He let out an exaggerated sigh. "Thank you for helping me see the light."

His sarcasm was infuriating. Not to mention his complete lack of shame. "Seriously, she's like . . . twenty-two."

Oscar nodded solemnly. "Yeah. You're right. I'm completely delusional."

"Apparently." I turned away, watching as Dad, Roland, and Sam began strolling down the boardwalk toward the theater. Jess kept pace at their side, camera steady on her shoulder. Mi Jin and Lidia trailed not far behind her. I set off after them without another word to Oscar.

His stupid crush on Mi Jin aside, it was pretty strange

58

that both the crew's camera *and* laptop had briefly malfunctioned. The laptop glitch came with a message. Mi Jin had said the camera glitch wasn't an error code—maybe it was a message, too. Sam said he sensed a presence, but not Red Leer . . . was it the show's ghost? The one so many fans seemed to think was behind the host curse and all the equipment glitches? I remembered the way Sam had stared at me a few minutes ago when the camera freaked out, and had a mental image of a ghost floating at my side.

Suddenly, I felt ridiculous. One day with a bunch of ghost hunters and I was already buying into the whole paranormal activity thing. Still . . .

When Jess called "Cut!" and started talking to Dad and the other guys, I hurried over to Mi Jin.

"Do you have a pen or anything?"

"Sure!" She dug a pencil out of the camera bag and handed it to me.

"Thanks." I turned away, quickly jotting down the second message under the first.

KEEP HER AWAY FROM THE MEDIUM
13 Xs

"What's that?" Mi Jin asked curiously, and I folded the paper and shoved it back into my pocket.

"Nothing important."

CHAPTER EIGHT
TEA PARTY OF THE DAMNED

P2P WIKI
Entry: "Dead Air"
[Last edited by Maytrix]

  "Dead air" refers to the approximately ninety seconds of dead air during the pilot episode of *Passport to Paranormal*, which took place at the Limerick Bed & Breakfast on the northern coast of Oregon. The disturbance occurred during the last ten minutes of airtime. Viewers suddenly lost audio and video during a scene showing the crew walking from the B&B to the nearby lighthouse. No one, including Fright TV, could explain the dead air. The episode resumed to show the crew back at the B&B, leading many fans to believe the missing footage took place in the lighthouse.

  To date, the crew refuses to discuss what happened in the lighthouse, nor will they share the footage. When asked for a possible explanation of the dead air, *P2P* creator and producer Lidia Bettencourt commented: "I guess it's just part of being the most haunted show on television." The phrase immediately became the show's unofficial slogan, an idea supported by the crew's frequent tech glitches and apparent inability to keep a host (for more, see: The Host Curse).

MY post-dinner nap attempt was a success—a solid hour of blissful unconsciousness. I rolled over and stared at the clock: 8:31 p.m. Yeah, there was no way I was going to sleep normally tonight.

Both Dad and his laptop were gone, but he'd left one of his key cards behind. I vaguely remembered Jess saying something at dinner about a meeting that night in the hotel's conference room. Slipping on a pair of shoes, I grabbed Dad's key to the room the crew was using to store equipment. Maybe there was an extra laptop in there I could use.

A minute later, I swiped the key to room 301, then pushed the door open a crack. "Hello?" I stuck my head inside. The room was deserted.

Both beds and the floor were covered in camera bags and cables, mics and tripods, thermal scanners and EMF detectors. Propping the door open behind me, I scanned the room quickly and spotted a closed laptop next to the TV. "Hallelujah," I whispered, hurrying over and pulling up a chair. I opened the laptop, powered it on, and waited impatiently for it to load.

And waited. And waited.

I frowned, tapping my fingers on the table. This show seriously needed some better equipment. Finally, the desktop appeared. But before I could click on anything, a video popped up and began to play.

"Are you ready?"

I recognized Sam's voice immediately. The camera sat perfectly still at eye level—on a tripod, I figured—in front of a tiny table in a cramped, circular room. Sam sat between Lidia and a blond, round-faced woman wearing a ton of makeup—Emily Rosinski, the first host. All three were holding hands. The only light came from a single, dim bulb over their heads.

Lidia nodded. "*Yes,*" she whispered.

I tapped the escape key several times, then held down the power button. Nothing. The video just kept playing.

Sam tilted his head back, his expression serene. "*Close your eyes,*" he instructed. Lidia obeyed immediately, but Emily continued to stare at him, her expression rapt. Sam started to speak so softly, I couldn't catch all the words.

"*We invite you to join . . . present, let us know you're . . . our energies, if you wish . . .*"

Lidia drew a slow, steady breath, her hands visibly trembling. Emily leaned closer to Sam. "*Are you sensing a presence?*" she said in a loud, exaggerated whisper.

Sam didn't respond. "*If you're willing . . . communicate, we ask that you . . . let Lidia know you're present . . .*"

I'd seen every episode of *Passport to Paranormal*, but this scene didn't look familiar. The bulb hanging overhead flickered once, very briefly. Emily gasped.

"*Did you see that, Sam?*" she cried shrilly. "*I think you've made contact!*"

I snorted. No wonder they'd never used this footage. Uber-cheesy.

Sam didn't even open his eyes. "*Focus, Emily,*" he said dreamily.

He continued murmuring, his voice barely audible. Lidia's breathing grew heavier and heavier, while Emily just gazed adoringly at Sam. The lightbulb flickered again, and she squirmed in her chair.

"Sam, I think—"

Suddenly, Lidia's eyes flew open. She sucked in a sharp breath just as the lightbulb exploded. Emily's shriek cut off abruptly.

I blinked in the sudden darkness, goose bumps breaking out all over my arms. The laptop had powered off, and the hotel room was pitch-black.

Heart thudding in my ears, I got to my feet. I hadn't turned on the lights when I came in, but I'd definitely left the door wide open.

Now it was closed.

"Hello?" I whispered. Feeling for the desk lamp, I flipped the switch. Nothing.

I felt a flicker of fear, quickly replaced by irritation. "Oscar," I said firmly, turning in a full circle. "Knock it off, this isn't funny."

No response.

I made my way slowly across the room, carefully navigating around the bags and coils of cables on the floor. Twice I paused and listened, but the room remained silent. When I reached the door, I yanked it open. Light from the hallway flooded the room. I spotted a light switch next to the bathroom door and flipped it on.

"Where are you hiding?" I muttered, poking my head inside the bathroom before checking the closet. "Oscar, come on . . ."

But he wasn't there. Hands on my hips, I stared at the laptop. Oscar must have been walking down the hall, seen me using the laptop, and shut the door. And the lamp . . .

Crossing the room, I flipped the lamp switch a few times. Then I saw the cord lying across the table. Someone's phone charger was plugged into the socket instead. Well, that explained that.

I shook my head, my relief mixed with annoyance. Apparently Oscar was determined to scare me. He could have set it up so that the video automatically started playing when someone turned the laptop on. Although . . .

How could he have fixed it so that the laptop turned off right when the bulb exploded in the video?

I shivered, remembering the creepy way Lidia's eyes had flown open. Before I could talk myself out of it, I powered the laptop back on and held my breath. The desktop looked normal—no videos, nothing unusual. I waited a few seconds, but nothing happened.

So that made three weird glitches: the printer, the camera, and the laptop. I sat down and opened the web browser. I wasn't ready to believe the glitches were all thanks to a restless spirit haunting the show, but at least now I had something to write about for my second blog post.

At a quarter to ten the next morning, I stumbled off the elevator and into the lobby. Mi Jin waved at me from where she sat curled up in an armchair with her laptop. "Morning!"

"Mmmph," I mumbled, eyeing the bagel in her hand. "Where'd you get that?"

She pointed to a door by the front desk. "Breakfast room."

"Thanks."

A few minutes later, I returned carrying a bagel smeared with grape jelly and a paper cup filled with chocolate milk. I started to take a sip as I sat in the chair next to Mi Jin, then yawned widely.

"You look dead," Mi Jin observed. "Bad night's sleep?"

"I don't think it qualified as sleep." I balanced my cup on the armrest and took a bite of bagel. "Where's everyone else?"

"Your dad and Jess went to check out Crimptown for tonight," she replied. "Roland might've gone with them, I'm not sure. Lidia's on the phone setting up stuff for Brussels next week. And Sam's having a tea party with Sonja Hillebrandt and the pirate who killed her."

I choked on my bagel, giggling. "He's *what*?"

Mi Jin grinned. "Sorry, that was mean. He's . . . you know, doing his medium thing. Trying to contact Sonja and Red Leer by sitting at a table in a dark room." She shrugged. "Whenever I watch someone conduct a séance, it reminds me of when I was little and I'd host tea parties for my imaginary friends."

I took another sip of chocolate milk. "So you don't believe in ghosts?"

Her eyes widened. "Oh, I totally believe. I just take a more technical approach than Sam."

"What do you mean?"

Mi Jin sat up a little straighter. "It takes a really high amount of energy for a ghost to do something big, like move a solid object or possess a person," she said seriously. "But they can affect electrical currents pretty easily. Like with white noise. If a ghost is speaking, your ears won't pick it up. But if you get an audio recording, you can isolate the voice in the white noise. It's called EVP—electronic voice phenomena. Same thing with photos—even if we can't see a ghost, a camera can capture its image because it detects a broader spectrum of energy than the human eye."

She paused, popping the last bite of bagel into her mouth. "So I try to use technology to communicate. It's not that I think Sam's way doesn't work, I just think my way has a higher possibility of success. You should see my electronic Ouija board."

"Seriously? Where'd you get that?"

"I made it," Mi Jin said proudly. "It's a regular Ouija board with some modifications."

I took a sip of chocolate milk. "So the camera yesterday . . . You're saying that could've been a ghost? Not that I think it was," I added hastily. "But I know a lot of fans think the show's haunted."

Mi Jin nodded. "Yeah, totally. That's why I recorded it happening."

"So you don't really think Oscar did it?"

"Nah. He's good with electronics, but I don't think he could've managed that."

"Me either." Propping my feet up on the coffee table, I tried to sound nonchalant. "Speaking of haunted equipment, I tried to use that laptop in room 301 last night, and it kind of freaked out."

Mi Jin tilted her head. "How so?"

"Started playing old footage of the show," I said. "And then it just weirdly shut off."

"Huh. What was the footage?"

I smiled. "A tea party. Just Sam, Lidia, and Emily."

"Which episode?"

"Dunno," I said with a shrug. "I've seen every episode, but I didn't recognize it. I figured it was footage they never used."

Mi Jin paused, lips pressed together like she was weighing her words. "Could you tell where they were?" she asked at last.

"Um . . . a really small room." I squinted, picturing the scene. "There were windows, but it was dark outside. They were sitting at a little table. It looked like the room was filled with junk, like maybe an attic. But the light was too dim to make anything out."

Actually, the image would have made a beautifully creepy photo, I thought. The bulb casting a yellowish light on three people huddled around a table holding hands, surrounded by shadowed boxes and objects, the night sky visible through the windows behind them . . . *Never use flash in low-light shots, Kat; you'll flatten the background . . . Use a higher ISO—it'll give you more contrast and depth . . .*

It was a few seconds before I realized Mi Jin was talking. "What?"

"Do you think maybe it was the missing lighthouse footage?" Mi Jin said, studying me over her coffee cup. "You know, the dead air from the first episode?"

I blinked. "Actually . . . maybe, yeah. It could've been a

lighthouse. Have you ever seen that footage?"

"Nope," Mi Jin replied. "But I do know that Sam had a tea party in the lighthouse. Originally, he was going to do one for every episode, but Jess made him stop after that one." She glanced around, lowering her voice. "I overheard Jess and Lidia arguing about it once. Lidia's *way* into tea parties. You know, because of her brother."

I frowned. "You mean Oscar's dad?"

"No, Lidia's twin," Mi Jin replied. "He died when they were teenagers."

My eyes widened. "How?"

"Heart condition," she said simply. "They were both born with it, but his was much worse than hers, apparently."

I remembered Lidia taking her pills yesterday and explaining about her pacemaker. "Oh."

"They grew up in Oregon," Mi Jin went on. "On the coast, really close to that lighthouse—that's why Lidia chose it for the first episode of *P2P*. She and her brother were totally obsessed with it when they were little, because it was abandoned, but sometimes the light would just start flashing, like it was trying to signal a ship. They were convinced it was haunted." Mi Jin shrugged. "Apparently Lidia got pretty worked up during the séance. It's not good for her health. So Jess convinced her to stop doing them on the show."

We sat in silence for a minute. I pictured Lidia seated at the table, so intent, so focused . . . the way her eyes had flown open just as the bulb exploded . . .

"Morning!" Mi Jin called. I glanced over as Oscar stepped off the elevator, eyes bloodshot, black hair sticking up in all directions. Mi Jin snickered. "Wow. Kat, looks like you're runner-up in the most beautiful zombie competition."

Oscar shuffled across the lobby to the breakfast room without a word. I shook my head. "Cheerful, isn't he?"

She smiled. "You two just got off on the wrong foot. He's a nice guy."

"If you say so."

Hearing about Lidia's childhood made me wonder yet again about Oscar's father. Why wasn't he living with him? I opened my mouth to ask Mi Jin, but closed it when Oscar returned, carrying a bowl of cereal and a plate stacked with what looked like a loaf's worth of toast. He flopped down on the sofa and crammed a piece of toast in his mouth, eyeing me.

"*Psycho*?"

I was offended for a split second before I realized he meant my Bates Motel T-shirt. "Oh. Yeah."

"All you wear is horror stuff," Oscar said dryly, and I gave him an icy stare.

"One of the perks of my mom leaving. I can wear what I want without getting harassed."

As soon as the words left my mouth, I felt a pang of guilt. After all, Oscar's mom had died. He'd been really young, according to Lidia, but it had still been an insensitive thing to say. And I had no idea what the deal was with his dad.

But Oscar didn't flinch. He just held my gaze, his expression inscrutable. After a few seconds of awkward silence, Mi Jin cleared her throat.

"The first time I saw *Psycho* was at a friend's sleepover

in seventh grade," she said, and Oscar finally looked away. "I hid my eyes through most of it. Same thing with *House on Haunted Hill.*"

"That's one of my favorites," I told her. "Apparently when I was in kindergarten, I went around telling everyone I was going to marry Vincent Price."

"You watched that movie in *kindergarten*?" Mi Jin said incredulously.

"My dad and grandma love horror movies. I grew up watching them."

"And you weren't scared?"

"Well, yeah, but in the fun way," I said. "There's the kind of scared you get from movies and stories, and then there's the real kind of scared. Two different things. Horror movies are the fun kind of scary."

"I guess that makes sense." Shaking her head, Mi Jin took a sip of coffee. "I can't believe you had a crush on Vincent Price. That's amazing. And a little frightening. Although now that I think about it," she mused, "I went through a serious obsession with Cruella De Vil when I was seven. I wore fake furs and tried to convince my mom to let me bleach my hair on the left side so it'd be black and white. Somehow the fact that Cruella wanted to kill puppies didn't register till later."

Oscar was staring at Mi Jin, wide-eyed. She grinned at him. "Problem?" Shaking his head silently, Oscar shoved the last piece of toast into his mouth. "No horror villain crushes for you?" Mi Jin added teasingly, causing Oscar to choke a little. I tried to hide my laughter behind my cup.

Clearing his throat, Oscar tossed his napkin on the table. "Thomas Cooper's coming," he said curtly.

Way to change the subject, I thought, wiping my eyes. "Who?"

"Fright TV executive vice president," Mi Jin explained. "He's meeting us in Brussels."

"Nope. He's getting in this afternoon," Oscar told her. "I heard Lidia on the phone with him this morning."

"Really? Oh boy." Mi Jin leaned back in her chair, chewing her lip.

"Is that a bad thing?" I asked.

"Yup." Oscar picked up his bowl of cereal. "My guess is that he's gonna cancel the show if the next episode's ratings aren't better."

"No way." Mi Jin shook her head vehemently. "We *just* got a new host—he's not going to cancel that fast."

Oscar shrugged. "That's not what it sounded like on the phone. Lidia said something about the Halloween episode being our last shot."

He sounded supremely unconcerned, but his mouth tightened a bit. I drummed my fingers on my armrest, trying not to look as worried as I felt.

"But that's the next episode we're shooting," Mi Jin said, forehead crinkled. "In Brussels. That one will air on Halloween."

Two episodes. Do the math. I grimaced, remembering the thread about the host curse on the *P2P* forums. It didn't matter if the curse was a publicity stunt or paranormal activity—all that mattered was that if it was real, then

Brussels would be Dad's last episode.

Mi Jin must have noticed my expression, because she nudged my leg with her boot. "Cheer up!" she said. "We'll find out what's going on when Thomas gets here. And hey, bonus—he usually brings his kids! They're probably on fall break right now. Jamie's around your age, and Hailey's in sixth grade."

I smiled, but I couldn't muster any enthusiasm. This wasn't fair—they weren't giving Dad a chance. If Thomas canceled the show after Brussels, we'd be back in Chelsea by the end of the month.

And the Thing would be waiting for me. So I had no intention of going back.

CHAPTER NINE
ATTACK OF THE
KiLLER RATINGS

From: timelord2002@mymail.net
To: acciopancakes@mymail.net
Subject: hey

Kat—I'm not supposed to be online (grounded again, like it's my
fault Trish brought Fang over and he decided to hide in our dryer
while Mom was doing laundry) but I had to tell you—yesterday
Trish's parents took us all out to dinner and we saw your
grandma. She was with your mom. I figured you'd want to know
about another sighting. Do you think she's moved back?

   I'm ungrounded this weekend. Maybe we can video chat or
something.—Mark

AFTER breakfast, I endured an entire hour of Oscar's dumb
jokes during a geography lesson with Mi Jin. Then we
read a creepy poem by Edgar Allan Poe, which would've
been awesome if it wasn't for Oscar adding his own stupid
commentary every other line. I was relieved when Mi Jin
gave us a few worksheets to do on our own so she could
meet up with the crew. Grabbing the sheets, I hurried back
to my hotel room for some quiet time.

   "Hey, Dad—oh, sorry," I whispered when he glanced up,
phone pressed against his ear.

"Yeah, I understand," Dad said, rubbing his forehead. "Well . . . that's up to you."

I flopped back on my bed, staring at Dad's reflection in the vanity mirror. He looked nervous. He *sounded* nervous. Which was weird, because Dad was a total pro when it came to stressful job stuff. If he was stressed, it had to be because of Thomas Cooper.

"Okay. Well . . . now's not a good time, honestly. I don't . . . Look, I'll let you know, okay? I've got to go." Dad hung up and sighed.

"Everything okay?" I asked tentatively.

"Hmm?" Dad blinked a few times, then smiled at me. "Yeah, fine. Lessons going all right?"

"Pretty good," I said. "Mi Jin's really cool. Oscar's obnoxious."

Dad laughed. "You'll be friends before you know it."

"No, we won't," I said flatly. "Why does everyone keep saying that?"

"You're right, sorry." Dad stood, slipping on his jacket. "You're clearly mortal enemies born to destroy one another. Neither can live while the other survives."

"Exactly." I watched as he slipped his room key into his pocket. "So . . . Thomas Cooper's coming today, huh?"

"Yup." Dad's expression didn't change as he headed for the door. "Around four, I think—you should come down to the lobby, I hear he's bringing his kids. See you in a bit!"

"Bye." The second the door clicked shut, I tossed my worksheets aside and grabbed Dad's laptop. I had to see what the *P2P* fans were saying now.

But when I opened the forum, the title of the newest thread

74

pushed all thoughts of the host curse out of my head.

Maytrix [admin]
Someone sent me a link to this blog . . . Looks like Jack's got a 13-yo daughter who's traveling with the show! Could be interesting. She's got a post up about the next episode in Rotterdam, which is pretty cool. But it's the second post you guys should check out—apparently the show's ghost is restless. Printer spitting out random messages, cameras going wonky, laptops turning off and on . . . great stuff! I kind of love that this girl's giving us a behind-the-scenes look.

skEllen [member]
OMG I <3 THIS!!!1!!

presidentskroob [member]
do you think fright tv knows about this blog? like, is she getting paid or something? could just be another stunt.

AntiSimon [member]
It's not a stunt. The show's haunted, that's why the equipment keeps freaking out.

YourCohortInCrime [member]
Yeah, that must be it. Couldn't have anything to do with the fact that electronics glitch out sometimes.

AntiSimon [member]
YCIC, sometimes I wonder why you even watch this show. You're not a believer.

YourCohortInCrime [member]
I watch because I want them to show me proof. THEN I'll believe.

And some kid whining about a broken laptop's not gonna do it.

beautifulgollum [moderator]
I wouldn't call it whining, YCIC. She seems like a smart girl to me. And it's great to have someone with the show blogging about this stuff!

spicychai [member]
too bad she'll be gone after the second episode. along with her dad.

I scrolled down the thread, then hopped over to my blog. Maytrix and AntiSimon had left comments on my last post: *"wow, thanks for sharing!"* and *"great posts, keep 'em coming!"* Grandma commented, too—*"Love it! Have you asked Sam about the messages? (And where are my pics??)"*

I clicked back over to the forums, relieved I hadn't described the video in detail in my post. I just said it was extra footage they never used. It wasn't my fault the video had started playing, but I kind of didn't want the rest of the crew to know I'd seen the lighthouse séance. After my chat with Mi Jin, I couldn't help wondering what the fans would think if I posted about what really happened during the dead air.

Watching the fans talk about me was bizarre, too. Most of them were nice, but the "some kid whining about a broken laptop" comment was pretty irritating. I didn't say it was *broken*, I said it started playing a random video before turning itself off. And I so did not *whine* about it. But that wasn't the comment that bothered me the most.

Too bad she'll be gone after the second episode. I pictured how stressed Dad had been on the phone just now. Roland said they did their best to make things *entertaining*—were they going to fire my dad as part of a publicity stunt?

At four o'clock, I leaned back and rubbed my eyes. I'd been poring over the *P2P* forums, looking for anything I could find about the curse and the former hosts. There was a lot. These fans were seriously chatty. I'd just clicked on yet another thread about Sam and Emily when I remembered Thomas Cooper had probably arrived.

A minute later, I stepped off the elevator and froze when someone shouted my name.

"Kat!" A round-faced girl ran toward me, her curly brown ponytail bouncing. "I'm Hailey Cooper and oh my God I think it's so *cool* that you started that blog about the show and is it really true that a ghost printed out a message for you and what did it *say*?"

Without waiting for a response, she threw her arms around me in a giant hug. Bewildered, I stared over her shoulder. Everyone in the lobby was watching.

"Everyone" included Dad, the entire crew, Oscar, a stern-looking man in a rumpled suit, and a boy my age with curly brown hair just like the girl currently wrapped around me like a spider monkey.

I cleared my throat. "Um . . . hi."

"Mr. Cooper, this is my daughter, Kat." Dad stepped forward, motioning me over. "Kat, apparently Hailey here is a fan of your blog."

"No kidding," I said dryly. Hailey giggled, pulling away so I could shake Mr. Cooper's hand.

"She's been blogging about the show for friends and family back home," Dad told Mr. Cooper, who nodded with this expression like he couldn't care less.

"That's nice," he said without giving me so much as a second glance. "Lidia, can we—"

"A bunch of fans found it, though!" Hailey interrupted, beaming at her father. "They *love* it!"

"It's true," her brother chimed in. "They linked it on the *P2P* boards."

Roland groaned. "Did they really?" I saw him and Jess exchange a look.

"They did, and a couple of them commented on her post!" Hailey informed him before turning back to me. "Seriously, though, what was the message? The first one, with the printer?"

"Um . . ." I could feel Oscar's eyes on me. I still wasn't entirely positive the printer hadn't been another one of his pranks. "Nothing, really. Just . . . gibberish."

"Oh." Hailey's face fell. "Still, though, it sounded so creepy, plus the camera thing—Mi Jin, did it really have thirteen *X*s?"

Mi Jin grinned. "It totally did."

"Awesome! Are you bringing the Ouija board to Crimptown tonight?" Hailey plowed on without pausing for breath. "Can we try it before you guys start filming? Did you tell Kat and Oscar about that time Jamie contacted that dead lady in the hotel in London? Jamie is *so* good at Ouija,

Kat. You've got to see it. It's *amazing*."

Stifling a laugh, I glanced at her brother. "It's true," he agreed, his expression as serious as Hailey's. "I'm the Ouija master." Then he smiled at me.

It was one of those happy smiles that makes you smile back like a reflex. And not that I'd thought he was bad-looking before or anything, but his whole face kind of lit up, and . . .

. . . it was a nice smile, that's all I'm saying.

"So, tonight maybe we can contact Sonja Hillebrandt!" Hailey exclaimed. "And Red Leer! See, I know the names and all about the history of Crimptown because—"

"Hailey," Mr. Cooper said with a sigh.

"Hold that thought, sweetie." Smiling, Jess ruffled Hailey's hair. "Tom, we've got the conference room all ready—should we meet you there in ten minutes?"

"Sounds good. I'll get our room key." As Mr. Cooper headed over to the desk, the rest of the crew filed slowly across the lobby. I snuck a glance at Dad, but his inner anchor had taken over—he didn't seem nervous at all. Everyone else looked a bit on edge, though. (Well, except for Sam, who wore his usual glazed "my mind is in the realm of the spirits" expression. He started wandering into the breakfast room until Roland grabbed his sleeve and led him down the hall.)

As soon as the adults were out of earshot, Oscar turned to me. "Why'd you lie?"

"Excuse me?"

"The message, the one that printed—you said it was a

bunch of gibberish. It wasn't."

"So you *did* type it up, then," I said triumphantly.

Oscar smirked. "Uh, no? You told me yesterday, right after the camera freaked out."

"Oh, right." *Dang.* I pressed my lips together, aware of Hailey and Jamie looking back and forth between us like this was a ping-pong match. "It's nothing. I just didn't want to bother Lidia and everyone else with it."

"So there really was a message? What did it say?" Hailey asked, her eyes round. Glancing over to make sure their father was still preoccupied, I pulled the paper from my pocket and unfolded it. Hailey, Jamie, and Oscar huddled in to read.

"*Keep her away from the medium,*" Hailey whispered slowly, tucking a stray curl behind her ear. "Whoa. So it's about Sam; he's the medium . . . who's the *her*?"

I shrugged. "No idea."

"And it wasn't on the screen? It just printed out?"

"Yeah."

"What's with thirteen *X*s?" Jamie asked, and I gave Oscar a sidelong look. But either he was innocent or he had a killer poker face.

"Camera malfunction," I said carefully. "It showed up on the viewfinder for a minute or two."

"This is *excellent!*" Hailey clapped her hands in delight. "You should add this to your blog post, Kat. Like, take a picture of it or something. Oh, oh, oh, you should take a camera down to Crimptown tonight, too!" she cried, and I felt a pang of longing at the thought of all the potential

80

eerie pictures. "I bet the fans would love to see photos before the episode comes on."

I laughed. "Fans? Like, two people from the forums left comments, that's it."

"Yeah, but . . ." Hailey's eyes darted over to her father.

Jamie cleared his throat. "We found your blog yesterday when they started talking about it in the forums, so we started hyping it up to Dad a little."

"A *lot*," Hailey corrected him. "Not that he listened. He never . . ." Jamie shot her a look and she fell silent, glowering.

"Why were you telling him about it in the first place?" I asked curiously.

"Well, because it could bring more fans in, and that couldn't hurt . . ." Jamie trailed off, looking uncomfortable.

Oscar shoved his hands in his pockets. "You think your dad's going to cancel the show, don't you."

Jamie winced. "Well . . . maybe. Fright TV is talking about making the Halloween episode the last one. They've got some new series about vampires they want to put in *P2P*'s time slot."

"But that's the next episode," I said, struggling to keep my voice low. "In Brussels."

"It's not definite yet," Jamie assured me. "That's what they're meeting about. When Dad called to tell Lidia, she swore they'd figure out a way to improve the ratings. And he said they'd have to try something new, because what they've been doing isn't working. So Hailey and I thought maybe your blog might be the 'something new' that saves the show."

I laughed dryly. "Thanks, but doubtful. That blog's really just for my grandma and a few friends."

"Let's go, kids!" Mr. Cooper was heading toward the elevator, pulling his suitcase behind him. "I promised your mom we'd call when we got in."

Jamie picked up his suitcase. "See you tonight?" he asked, looking from me to Oscar.

"Definitely," I said, and Oscar nodded. Jamie smiled, I smiled back—seriously, reflex—then he and Hailey followed their dad onto the elevator.

The doors slid closed, leaving Oscar and me alone in the lobby.

"It's over," he said, pulling an iPod out of his pocket. "Two episodes, then we're going home."

"Positive thinker, huh?"

"Just realistic." Oscar plopped down on one of the armchairs. "Can't run away from your mom forever."

It was a few seconds before his words sank in.

"*Excuse* me?" I stared at him until he looked up. "What do you know about my mother?"

Oscar shrugged. "Yesterday you said your mom left, and you seemed pretty bitter about it. If you go home, you'll have to deal with her getting . . ."

I crossed my arms. "Getting *what*?"

For a second, I could have sworn I saw a flicker of guilt in his expression. Then he rolled his eyes. "I don't know. Getting on your case about wearing all those stupid T-shirts?"

My mouth opened and closed a few times before I managed to speak. "How did you convince Lidia the reason you got expelled for fighting was because you were bullied?" I snapped. "Obviously it was the other way around."

Without giving him a chance to respond, I crossed the lobby and jabbed the elevator buttons, fuming all the way back to my room.

CHAPTER TEN
FROM BEYOND THE OUIJA BOARD

From: acciopancakes@mymail.net
To: trishhhhbequiet@mymail.net, timelord2002@mymail.net
Subject: stuff

I'm spending the night in the "haunted" tunnels tonight, so I figured I should send you guys one last e-mail before Red Leer gets me.

Mark—sorry you got grounded. And I'm pretty sure there's no way they'd let me actually be on the show. Trish—I haven't gotten to see much of Rotterdam yet, but the waterfront is really pretty. The cast and crew are cool—especially Mi Jin. You'd both love her. (Mark, she brought a huge backpack filled with nothing but comic books; she's totally obsessed. Maybe even more than you, if that's possible.) Lidia's nephew Oscar is with us, too. He's our age, but he's really annoying. Too bad.

The executive VP of Fright TV is here and he brought his kids—I just met them. Jamie's thirteen and Hailey's eleven, and they're really nice. They're both WAY into the show, and they found my blog. They think just because a few *P2P* fans from the forums like it, maybe the ratings will get better. Aaaand they said the network's probably going to cancel the show after the Halloween episode. So. That's not good.

So, you guys saw my mom out with Grandma the other night? That's the third sighting since August. I bet she thadfewfwidskefaszaaaaaaaaaaaaaaaaaaaaaaaaaaaaaa woke up with my cheek pressed against Dad's laptop. Blinking, I stared blearily at the screen. Apparently I'd ended up face-planting on the keyboard. Through my sleep haze, I noticed the sticky notes with the hotel's logo printed along the bottom. On the top was a message in Dad's neat script.

Heading down to Crimptown early. Everyone's meeting in the theater lobby next door at nine—if you'd rather stay in tonight, call Lidia's cell to let me know. The front desk can connect you. If you do come, bring your camera! Grandma would love to see some pics. :)

Stay in my room while everyone else spends the night in a haunted tunnel system beneath Rotterdam? Sorry, Dad, that's not why I signed up for this adventure. I shot to my feet, staring at the clock—five to nine. Dad had placed the Elapse out on the dresser where I couldn't miss it.

Mirror check: My hair was smashed flat on the right side, sticking up on the left side. My eyes were pink and glazed over. Sweet. Nothing in the tunnels could possibly look any scarier than me.

There was no time to shower, so I swiped on some deodorant and swapped Bates Motel for the least wrinkled T-shirt in my suitcase (Zombies Are People, Too!). Four minutes later, I burst through the theater's front doors, still trying to smooth down my hair. Normally I'd just braid it, but that wasn't exactly an option now that it didn't even reach my shoulders. At some point I'd have to figure out another way to keep it out of my face.

Dad and the rest of the crew were deep in discussion

with a guy I didn't recognize, surrounded by tons of equipment. Not far from them, Oscar stood talking to Jamie and Hailey. He said something that made them laugh, and I felt a sudden flash of irritation. Did Oscar get along with *everyone* except me?

"What's with the roar face?" Mi Jin appeared at my side, looping a cable around her arm into a neat coil.

I tore my eyes off Oscar and the Coopers. "What?"

"You look pretty ticked off."

"Oh." I shrugged. "It's nothing."

"Okay," Mi Jin said easily. "So, are you excited about tonight? I brought the Ouija board!"

"Cool! Do you use it on the show?"

"Oh, no way," she replied. "It's just for you guys. You've got to stay off camera, you know. Figured I'd bring some entertainment in case you get bored."

"Ah." I glanced over at the Coopers again, and this time, Hailey spotted me.

"Over here, Kat!" she yelled, waving wildly. Jamie waved, too, and I found myself wishing I'd spent that extra minute putting a comb to good use.

"Well, go over there," Mi Jin said, nudging my arm. "Don't be shy."

I snorted. "I'm not shy. I just figure I'm about to spend the whole night around Oscar—no reason to start any earlier than necessary." Mi Jin pursed her lips together like she was trying not to smile, and I sighed. "What?"

"Well . . ." She finished looping the cable and carefully pulled the coil off her arm. "That's pretty much what he said about you right before you got here."

"*What?*" Turning, I glared at Oscar, but he was too busy blabbing away with Jamie and Hailey to notice. "See? I *told* you he was a jerk. I can't—"

"Hang on there, Miss Hypocrite," Mi Jin teased, zipping her camera bag closed. "You said the same thing, after all."

"Who's a hypocrite?" Roland appeared at Mi Jin's side, sucker sticking out of his mouth. "This one?" He gave me a pointed look, and I scowled.

"Kat and Oscar got off to a bad start," Mi Jin informed him. "They think they don't like each other." I opened my mouth, but Roland beat me to it.

"Wrong," he said, taking the camera bag from Mi Jin. "They really *don't* like each other."

I blinked in surprise. "Yeah, we don't."

Mi Jin sighed. "But why not? You're so much alike!"

"That's exactly why." Crunching his sucker, Roland grinned at me. "Something wrong?"

"Um . . . Oscar and I are *not* alike," I said, vaguely aware that my voice had risen in both volume and pitch. "At *all*."

Roland studied me for a moment. "I bet your last report card was all Bs."

Taken aback, I glanced at Mi Jin. "Did you tell him that?" I asked, and she shook her head. Roland pulled the sucker out of his mouth and smiled.

"You're smart but you don't study," he told me. "You figure why bother when you know you can at least pass, right? You usually take charge when you're in a group— teachers like you because they think you're a leader, but the real reason you do it is you'd rather delegate the work than actually do it yourself. You get along fine with almost everyone, but you have very few friends you really trust. And if someone betrays that trust, you're done—no second chances."

He smiled smugly before popping the sucker back in his mouth. Mi Jin let out a low whistle.

"How'd you know all that?" she asked Roland, clearly impressed. He shrugged.

"Back when I was a therapist, I could diagnose new patients before they finished introducing themselves," he replied. "And everything I just said about her? Oscar's exactly the same."

Mi Jin's eyes widened. "Seriously? Whoa."

"Wait, just . . . hang on," I sputtered, my face hot. "That doesn't make sense."

"Sure it does," Roland replied. "It's obvious you both have trust issues. You're classic cases."

"Not the trust thing. You said Oscar and I don't like each other because we're *alike*," I said loudly. "And let's just—let's just pretend you got it all right, everything you said. Why wouldn't I like someone who was just like me?"

Roland flashed his purple-toothed grin. "Aha. *Now* you're thinking like a psychologist."

"All right, guys, we're moving!" Jess called. Roland winked at me before heading over to the rest of the crew, and once again I had no idea if he was mocking me.

Mi Jin thumped me on the back, laughing. "Look at you, all shell-shocked. Was that stuff really true?" I shoved my hands in my jacket pockets without responding, and her eyebrow ring shot up. "Well, I guess that answers that."

I hung back as the crew gathered around the guy I now realized was wearing a Crimptown tour guide T-shirt. Jess had her camera on as the guide chatted with Dad, but I barely heard a word.

The truth was, Roland nailed it. It was weird—beyond weird—to hear someone just sum me up like that. Especially when I hadn't even thought about most of it. I mean, yeah, when teachers split the class into groups, I usually took charge of mine. But I wasn't pushy or anything. Actually, the way Roland said it made me sound kind of lazy. *Student achieves below apparent ability.* I got that comment on report cards a lot. But whatever—my grades were good enough. What difference would a few points higher really make?

And as much as I hated to admit it, Roland was dead-on about the trust thing. I'd always had lots of friends, but there were only a handful of people I really, truly trusted. Right now it was down to Dad, Grandma, Trish, and Mark.

If someone betrays that trust, you're done. No second chances.

That part was 110 percent accurate, too. I mean, if someone you trust betrays you, why would they deserve another chance? You can forgive them, but you can't force yourself to trust them again.

"Hi, Kat!" Hailey said in a stage whisper. I looked up, startled to find her at my side.

"Hi," I whispered back, struggling not to try flattening my hair again when I noticed Jamie right next to her. Oscar had followed them over, and while his gaze was fixed on the crew, I could tell he was listening. "So, you guys have done this before?" I asked. "Spent the night in a haunted place while they film?"

Hailey nodded enthusiastically. "Four times! The haunted hotel in London was my favorite."

"What about your dad?" I asked, glancing around. Hailey rolled her eyes.

"He's back in our room, of course," she muttered. "We always ask him to come, but . . ." She shrugged.

"We usually find a place to camp out," Jamie added softly. "Jess doesn't like us too close to the cameras."

"Mi Jin brought the Ouija board," I said, nudging his elbow. "After all the big talk earlier, you'd better introduce me to some ghosts."

"Just you wait."

And there was that smile again. Jamie didn't just smile with his mouth—he smiled with his whole face. His nose crinkled, his eyes brightened like he was about to laugh, even his ears seemed to stick out a little more. (And they already stuck out quite a bit. Which was fairly adorable.)

The guide started moving toward the theater's bar, and the crew followed, Jess's camera still rolling. Dad stood next to her, listening intently to the guide. I caught his eye and gave him a thumbs-up, and he grinned. Well, he *looked* confident. Maybe the meeting with Thomas Cooper had been okay after all.

Of course, Dad was a pro at pretending nothing was wrong, even when everything was falling apart.

Crimptown was a labyrinth of tunnels made of crumbling gray brick and moldy wooden planks. Rusting pipes hung low overhead, occasionally dripping what I chose to pretend was water, despite its yellowish color, on the hard-packed dirt floor. Each tunnel had a few small storage rooms with rusty barred doors, which Red Leer had used as cells to lock up the men he kidnapped until he could smuggle them to his ship.

According to the guide, Crimptown only spanned about a dozen city blocks, but the complex system of winding narrow tunnels was several kilometers long, connecting all the theaters, hotels, restaurants, and anyplace else with a bar on the waterfront. Dim bulbs hung from the ceiling, and long, wooden slides marked the spots directly below the bars. The crew all shined their flashlights up the first one we'd seen, illuminating the trapdoor overhead. It was pretty horrifying to imagine all those poor guys getting thrown down the slides, waking up a prisoner in one of these dark, depressing cells.

Two hours, five rat sightings, and countless stubbed toes later, Jess lowered the camera and stretched her arms.

"Time to set up camp," she announced. "Mi Jin, Sam, Roland, we need more footage of the trapdoors—seems like the best place for Sam to start trying to make contact. Jack, Lidia, we'll take the EMFs and start checking out the cells."

Dad glanced at me. "And the kids . . . stay in a cell?"

"Jamie and Hailey know the drill," Lidia assured him.

"No splitting up, no exploring unless it's with an adult, and everyone gets one of these." Rummaging through her backpack, Lidia pulled out a few walkie-talkies. "No goofing around with them," she added, giving Oscar a pointed look.

"Goofing around how?" Oscar asked innocently.

Lidia smiled as she handed me a walkie-talkie. "Oh, I don't know . . . adding your own sound effects while we're filming, maybe?"

Oscar stuffed his walkie-talkie in his pocket. "Amateur stuff. I can do better than that," he told her.

I rolled my eyes as we followed Mi Jin into one of the cells. "Because masks and rubber snakes aren't amateur?" I muttered. Oscar ignored me.

"All right, gather round," Mi Jin said cheerfully, plopping down on the dirt and unzipping her backpack. Jamie and Hailey immediately sat on either side of her, and I knelt down next to Jamie, doing my best to avoid a damp spot from the leaky pipes. Oscar sat cross-legged between Hailey and me just as Mi Jin pulled something out of her bag and set it in the center of our circle with a flourish. "Ta-da!"

"Wow." I leaned forward, staring at the Ouija board.

YES   NO
ABCDEFGHIJKLM
NOPQRSTUVWXYZ
1234567890
GOOD BY E

Mi Jin had attached a small, square circuit board along the top between *YES* and *NO*. A thin cord connected the circuit board to a mouse, which was embedded in the center of a wooden teardrop-shaped planchette. At the tip of the planchette was a small, circular lens.

"Why's it all . . ." Oscar waved his hand at the board. "Computerized?"

"Moving solid objects takes a lot of energy for ghosts—electricity's easier to manipulate," Mi Jin explained, flipping a switch on the circuit board. It hummed to life, the tiny lightbulb flashing green. "You use it just like a regular Ouija board."

"The electrical current helps them move the planchette," Jamie added. "Much better chance of communication."

Oscar looked about as skeptical as I felt. Our eyes met for a second, and his lips quirked up. I ducked my head to hide my grin.

Mi Jin looked amused. "We've got a couple of nonbelievers here," she informed Jamie and Hailey. "I'm counting on you two to change their minds."

"You don't believe in ghosts?" Hailey asked me, wide-eyed.

"Um . . ." I sat back on my heels, thinking carefully. I didn't want to offend her or Jamie. "I guess I just need to see proof before I believe something's real."

Hailey nodded, turning to Oscar. "You too?"

Oscar shrugged. "Something like that."

Laughing, Mi Jin stood and brushed the dirt off her jeans. "Try *exactly* like that. Just one of the many things Kat and Oscar have in common. Right, Kat?" She winked at me on her way out of the cell.

"So who are we contacting?" I said quickly, before Oscar could ask what Mi Jin was talking about.

"Sonja Hillebrandt," Hailey replied immediately, her cheeks flushed with excitement. "She's the nice one. Red Leer was evil."

"Good call," I said. "No evil pirates invited to this party."

"Oh no, I totally want to contact him, too!" Hailey pulled a small notepad and a red pen from her pocket and set them next to the board. "Angry ghosts have more energy, so it's a little easier. But Sonja's the hero, right? She sacrificed her life to save her brother and all those prisoners. It's only polite to invite her first."

I couldn't help smiling at her enthusiasm. "You're not scared at all, huh?"

Jamie shook his head. "Nothing scares her."

"True," Hailey agreed, flipping the notepad open. "Oh, Kat! Do you still have that piece of paper you've got with the other messages? Can I use that instead?"

"Sure." I pulled the square of paper out of my back pocket and handed it over. Hailey unfolded it, smoothing it out on the dirt. Jamie adjusted the Ouija board, then took the planchette and set it in the center.

"Ready?"

"Why not."

He and Hailey placed the tips of their fingers along the edge of the planchette. Oscar and I followed suit.

"So, I'll try to contact Sonja," Jamie explained. "Hailey'll write down any responses we get. We all have to focus on Sonja. Maybe try picturing her, like that portrait from your blog post," he added to me. "Okay?"

"Sure," I said, and Oscar shrugged again. The four of us stared at the board. When the planchette immediately started to move, I looked up at Jamie. "You're doing that," I blurted out, then cringed at how accusatory I sounded.

Jamie smiled without taking his eyes off the planchette. "This is how we get started—like a warm-up. We'll move the planchette around until Sonja takes over." He cleared his throat. "Sonja Hillebrandt . . . please join us. We'd like to ask you a few questions. We invite you to talk with us."

As he spoke, we continued moving the planchette in slow circles across the board. I pressed my lips together, trying not to giggle at Hailey's dead-serious expression. Jamie cleared his throat.

"Remember, everyone needs to focus on *Sonja*," he said quietly. I chanced a peek at him. His gaze was still fixed on the planchette, but the corners of his mouth twitched. The urge to laugh increased, and I bit hard on the inside of my cheek.

Nearly a full minute passed with the four of us sitting in the dingy cell in silence, scraping a computer mouse stuck in a wooden plank across a board. The whole thing seemed more and more absurd with every second.

"Ooookay," Oscar said at last. "No offense, but this is—"

"It's not working because you aren't focusing on Sonja," Hailey interrupted. Her tone was terribly patient, as if she were talking to a toddler. I started snickering—I couldn't help it—and she turned to me. "You too, Kat! You have to *focus*."

Her schoolteacher voice and stern expression just made me laugh harder. "Sorry," I said, ducking my head. "It's just . . . Has this really *worked* for you guys before?"

Hailey nodded. "Yeah! We contacted our grandfather right after his funeral."

The laughter died in my throat. "Oh, I didn't realize," I said, flustered.

"It's okay," Jamie said quickly. "It was a couple of years ago. And it was just a regular Ouija board. But we definitely talked to him."

"Why are you so sure it worked?" Oscar asked.

"We asked him a few yes-or-no questions first," Hailey replied, tapping on the board. "Stuff only he would know. And then we asked where his pocket watch was."

"His watch?"

"It belonged to his father," Jamie explained. "Kind of a family heirloom. And after the funeral, we couldn't find it anywhere. Our mom was going nuts looking—she kept blaming herself for losing it."

"So we used the board to ask Grandpa," Hailey said in a low, conspiratorial voice. "And the planchette spelled out *J-A-R*."

"And you found the watch in a jar?" Oscar said. To his credit, he seemed to be making an attempt at not sounding too disbelieving.

"Nope." Hailey's eyes sparkled. "We looked in all the jars we could find, but no watch. And then we realized Grandpa just hadn't finished the word."

"Our mom interrupted us," Jamie added. "She got really freaked out when she saw us using the Ouija board—she hates these things. She made us get rid of that one, actually. Anyway, she walked in right after we got to the *R*."

"So what word did you think your grandpa was trying to spell?" I asked.

"Jared," Hailey said. "Our uncle—Mom's brother. Turns out he was going to *sell* the watch."

Oscar looked dubious. "He actually had it?"

Jamie nodded. "Yeah. We told Mom, and . . . Well, like I said, she hates Ouija boards, so at first she didn't want to listen to us. But Jared was at the funeral, obviously, and that was the last time we saw the watch, because Mom had laid it out on a table with some family photos and other stuff of Grandpa's, and . . ."

"It wasn't the first time Uncle Jared did something like that," Hailey said sadly. "Mom always calls him the black sheep of the family."

"He and Mom don't exactly get along," Jamie finished. "So she went and confronted him about the watch. She got it back, but they haven't spoken since then."

"You see?" Hailey said, sitting up straighter. "Proof. Grandpa told us where to find the watch."

I exchanged a glance with Oscar. I had to admit, it was a good story. But I wouldn't call it *proof*.

"I don't think they're convinced just yet," Jamie told Hailey with a sigh.

"Not quite." Leaning forward, I placed my fingers back on the planchette. "But I'm getting there. Convince me."

Grinning, Jamie reached for the planchette. Hailey and Oscar did, too, and we fell silent.

This time, I focused on Sonja.

I pictured her dark hair, her pale face, her delicate smile. I imagined her swapping her dress for her brother's clothes, tucking her hair up into a cap and hiding a knife under her coat. Sitting on a bar stool, fake-sipping a drugged drink, pretending to pass out, getting thrown through a trapdoor, sliding down, down, down until she hit the dirt floor, then whipping out her knife and running through the tunnels, sprinting toward this very cell—

The planchette twitched.

I barely managed to stop myself from pulling my fingers away. No one said anything, but I could tell they all felt it, too. Hailey leaned forward, staring intently at the board. Jamie closed his eyes. I glanced at Oscar, wondering if this was another prank. If so, it was a pretty mean one, considering how seriously Jamie and Hailey took this.

The planchette twitched again, then slid over until the lens magnified the letter *H*. I squinted at Oscar's fingers—it didn't *look* like he was moving the planchette, but I couldn't tell for sure. An *E* followed, then *L* . . . It slid away briefly before heading back to *L*. Then, slowly, the planchette scraped across the board to the left side, stopping on *O*.

"Hello." Jamie's voice, though soft, made me jump. "Is this Sonja?"

As the planchette crept across the board to *YES*, I glanced over at Oscar. His brow was furrowed, no trace of a smile on his face. Leaving two fingers on the planchette, Hailey reached over and picked up her pen.

"Hi, Sonja," Jamie said calmly. "Thank you for joining us. How many spirits are present right now, including you?"

The planchette moved down to the line of numbers, where the lens settled over *3*.

Jamie nodded. "Three. Thank you. Can you tell us who they—"

The planchette jerked violently, and Jamie fell silent. Our hands all moved quickly across the board as the lens magnified letters: *G–A–T–H–E* . . .

"Are you doing this?" I whispered to Oscar. He just shook his head without looking up.

Hailey carefully wrote down letter after letter, whispering each one under her breath. The planchette fell still at last, and she held the paper up for us to read:

G A T H E R T H E W O M E N

"Gather the women . . ." I chewed my lip. "That's what Sonja did, right? She gathered a bunch of women to—"

Before I could finish, the planchette jerked beneath my fingers again. The four of us stared as it scraped across the board. *F–R–E–E–T–H–E–M—NO*.

Jamie cleared his throat. "Sonja, are you still there?" The planchette twitched, then slid back over *NO*. "Who are we speaking to?"

The little green light on the circuit board started to flicker. I held my breath as the planchette began to move again.

L–E–E–R

"Wait, hold on," Hailey breathed, her handwriting getting messier as she scribbled down the new letters. "Ask about the third ghost. Sonja said there's three here."

Jamie nodded. "Is there another—"

The planchette jerked up to *YES*, then immediately zoomed over to *NO* before heading back to the letters. *F–R–E–E–T–H* . . . It paused, twitching.

"What's the deal?" Hailey asked, pen still poised over the paper.

"I think they're both trying to answer," Jamie said quietly. "Red Leer and whoever the third ghost is, they're both trying to control it."

Oscar and I shared a look. He wasn't buying this any more than me, I could tell. Not that I thought the Coopers were moving the planchette on purpose to trick us. They clearly *believed* they were communicating with ghosts . . . but that didn't make it true. If Jamie and Hailey knew their uncle was the kind of guy who'd steal his dead father's pocket watch, maybe spelling out their suspicions on a Ouija board had been easier than admitting it out loud.

I glanced down when the planchette lurched again.

K–E–E–P–H–E–R–A–W–A . . .

"*Keep her away*," Hailey said excitedly, still scribbling. "*From* . . . Kat, this is the same message that printed the other day! *Keep her away from the medium!*" She waved the paper at me, and I let go of the planchette to take it.

The green light flickered faster . . . then stopped. The planchette fell still, and Hailey groaned.

"Did the batteries die?"

Before anyone could respond, a distant crash caused us all to jump. A split second later, a scream echoed through the tunnels.

Hailey leaped to her feet first. She was halfway to the cell door when Jamie grabbed her wrist.

"What are you doing?" Hailey yelled, trying to tug her arm away. "Someone might've gotten hurt, we should—"

"You know the rules." Jamie's voice cracked a little. "We can't just go running around looking for them. Dad would flip out. We don't even know where they are. We'd get lost."

Hailey opened her mouth to retort, but Oscar waved his walkie-talkie at her. "That's why we've got these, right?" Without waiting for a response, he held it up to his mouth. "Aunt Lidia? Is everyone okay?"

My heart pounded in my ears as we waited for a response. Ghosts aside, there were plenty of ways someone could get hurt in the tunnels. The last thing Dad needed was a broken leg or something. After a few seconds of silence, I pulled out my own walkie-talkie, cramming the paper back in my pocket. "Dad?" I said, trying to sound calm. "Mi Jin? Is anyone there?"

For a moment, there was nothing but a soft crackle. Then someone spoke, but it didn't sound like Dad or anyone else on the crew. The voice was distant and echoey, like a soft whisper in a large hall. But the words were very clear.

"Help her."

The four of us stood frozen, staring at the walkie-talkie. Then Hailey wrenched her arm out of Jamie's grasp and sprinted into the tunnels.

CHAPTER ELEVEN
DEAD WOMAN WALKING

P2P WIKI
Entry: "Possession"
[Last edited by AntiSimon]

   Possession refers to a ghost or spirit taking control of a person's body, including motor and cognitive functions. To date, *P2P* has not recorded or reported such an event.

I raced after Jamie, Oscar right behind me. I could just make out Hailey's curly brown ponytail as she whipped around a corner. Seconds later, Jamie stopped so abruptly, I slammed into him.

"Which way?" he said frantically. Rubbing my shoulder, I squinted in the dim light and realized we were at a fork in the tunnel. "Which way did she go?"

"I don't know." I took a deep breath. "Um, try your walkie-talkie again."

Jamie fumbled with his walkie-talkie. "Hello? Jess, Mi Jin . . . anyone there?"

I swallowed hard, willing my pulse to slow down. Maybe I didn't believe in ghosts, but between the Ouija board, the dark tunnels, and that creepy voice . . . Well, being a *little* freaked out was understandable.

After a few seconds of static-filled silence, Jamie let out a frustrated groan. "Nothing. Should we—"

THUD.

A cry of pain ripped through the air, and goose bumps broke out all over my arms. Without a word, the three of us raced down the path on the left, toward the noise. I heard shuffling sounds around the corner, and voices—one familiar voice in particular . . .

"Dad!"

"Look out!"

Jamie went flying through the air in front of me, landing hard on the dirt. I managed to skid to a halt right in front of the thing that had tripped him. When I realized it was Jess lying on the ground, a scream rose up in my throat. I leaped backward into Oscar just as Jess sat up with a sigh. *"Cut!"*

Relief flooded through me as my eyes adjusted. Roland lowered the camera and hurried over to help Jamie while Dad pulled a very irritated-looking Jess to her feet. Behind them, a huge sack lay on the ground in front of one of the trapdoor slides.

"What happened?" I asked. "We heard screaming—"

"Flour," Roland interrupted, kicking the sack. "Or sugar, I'm not sure. Came shooting down the slide and knocked Jess over."

I watched Jess angrily swipe dirt off her jeans. "Are you okay?"

"Yeah, fine," she muttered. "That was *great* footage, and now we can't even use it."

"Why not?"

"Because you three can't be in the show," Dad said with a sigh, and I winced. "You got in the shot when you came barreling in here. Are you okay?"

"Yeah. Sorry."

Roland stared up at the trapdoor. "How long have you guys been wandering around, anyway? Did you do this?"

"We haven't . . ." I hesitated, confused. "Do what?"

Nudging the sack with his toe, Roland glanced at Oscar. "This. As a joke. Because Jess could've been seriously hurt."

Oscar's eyes widened. "What? I didn't—"

"We've been with Oscar the whole time," I interrupted, glaring at Roland. "We were in the cell and there was a crash and someone screamed. Hailey ran off, and we all went after her, but we lost her, and—"

"You *lost* her?" Without waiting for a response, Jess whipped out her walkie-talkie. "Lidia? Sam? You there?"

Roland groaned, rubbing his forehead. "We lost the network VP's daughter. Perfect."

"Hello?" Mi Jin's voice crackled through the walkie-talkie, and we fell silent.

"Mi Jin, do you have Hailey?" Jess said immediately.

"Um . . . yeah, she's right here with me." Everyone let out a collective breath, and Jamie's shoulders slumped in relief. *"But I can't . . . I . . ."*

Mi Jin's voice was breathy and strange. "Are you okay?" Jess asked, brow crinkled. "Is Lidia with you? Mi Jin?" No response, just a long, crackly silence.

Jess lowered the walkie-talkie. "Okay, let's find them. And we need to keep filming." She held her hand out, and

104

Roland handed her the camera. "Jack, can you take these guys back to the cell, please? Roland, come with me."

Jamie shook his head. "But Hailey—"

"I'll get her, and then the four of you are going back to the hotel," Jess said shortly. "We can't afford to throw away any more footage." With that, she set off down the tunnel with Roland, speaking in hushed tones.

Dad turned to Jamie, who was rubbing his elbow. "Do you need the first-aid kit?"

Jamie shook his head. "I'm fine."

Guilt burned in my chest as we followed Dad through the narrow tunnel. What if we'd ruined his first episode? Then again, no one could possibly expect us to just sit in the cell when people were screaming bloody murder and the walkie-talkies weren't working . . .

"Help her!"

I stopped cold, staring at my walkie-talkie. Dad glanced at me over his shoulder. "Something wrong?"

"Didn't you hear . . ." I paused, looking from Oscar to Jamie. They both stared at me blankly. "Um . . . never mind."

We continued down the tunnel. Had I imagined the voice? Probably, I told myself. Crimptown was creepy, it was the middle of the night, we'd been playing Ouija . . .

There had to be a logical explanation. Just like there had to be an explanation for the sack of flour that had knocked Jess over, and Mi Jin's strange, breathy voice. An explanation that did *not* involve the show's so-called ghost.

I frowned as another thought occurred to me. Jess was pretty irritated that we'd messed up her footage of the flour sack. And Roland had been quick to accuse Oscar of setting it up. But maybe that was just a cover. Maybe this was all just part of them "making things entertaining."

Or maybe I was trying too hard to pretend something genuinely supernatural wasn't happening here.

"Jack?"

The four of us spun around. Mi Jin peered out from behind the bars of one of the cells, her eyes glassy. And behind her . . .

"Hailey!" Jamie hurried forward and pulled on the bars, then the latch. "It's locked," he said in disbelief, standing back to let Dad try. "Why is it locked?"

Dad frowned, squinting at the latch. "It's not locked, just stuck," he said, tugging on it. "Mi Jin, what's going on? Why aren't you with Lidia and Sam?"

Hailey stepped up to the bars, too, rubbing her eyes. "What happened?" Jamie said urgently, grabbing her hand through the bars. "How'd you end up in here?"

Mi Jin tilted her head, watching as Dad continued yanking at the rusty latch. "I'm not sure. Sam was trying to contact Sonja, I had the camera, Lidia went to get . . . something . . ." She blinked, shaking her head. "It's weird, I can't remember anything after Lidia left."

Dad asked question after question, the screechy sounds from his war with the latch drowning out every other word. Jamie stood pressed up against the bars, still gripping Hailey's hand. It was eerie how dazed both girls were. Neither could remember how they'd ended up in the cell. I still wasn't sure what to think about the voice on the walkie-talkie or the flour sack, but Mi Jin definitely wasn't faking this. Her handheld camera hung forgotten at her side.

Quietly, I pulled the paper from my pocket and unfolded it. The bright red letters in Hailey's increasingly messy print stood out beneath my handwriting.

KEEP HER AWAY FROM THE MEDIUM
13 Xs
H E L L O
Is this Sonja?—YES
How many spirits?—3
G A T H E R T H E W O M E N
F R E E T H E M—NO
Is Sonja here?—NO
Who is this?—L E E R
Third ghost here?—YES/NO
F R E E T H—(Leer & ghost #3 fighting?)
K E E P H E R A W A Y F R O M T H E M E D I U M

I frowned. *Gather the women.* Jess had been knocked over by a sack of flour. Mi Jin and Hailey were locked in a cell. And Lidia had apparently disappeared. So far, Crimptown didn't seem to like us girls very much.

My neck tingled, and I spun around, staring down the tunnel. No one was there. Except . . .

Wiping my palms on my jeans, I took a step down the path, then another. Dad didn't notice—he was too busy trying to get the latch to open. But Oscar grabbed my arm.

"What are you doing?" he whispered, and I pointed.

"Do you see that?"

Oscar glanced down the tunnel. "See what?"

"A light," I said. "Well, not a light . . . it's kind of a glow." Ignoring the weird look he gave me, I took a few more steps. I opened my mouth to call out for Lidia, then closed it. Because this light wasn't from a flashlight. It was soft blue, and it rippled like water.

"Kat," Dad said, and the light vanished. I whirled around. "Where do you think you're going?"

"No, I—I thought I saw a light down there," I replied, feeling foolish. "It could be Lidia or Sam."

"We'll find them as soon as I get this latch open." Dad turned back to the cell door. "Stay here." The screeching resumed, and I waited a few seconds before I took a tentative step forward. Oscar shot me a questioning look, but I just shook my head. And when I took off, he didn't say a word.

Well, score one for Oscar. At least he knew when to keep his mouth shut.

I crept down the path as fast as I could, hardly daring to breathe. Dad would kill me for sneaking off—*if* I was sneaking off. But I was just going to the end of this tunnel. I'd seen some sort of light, I was sure of it. Keeping my hand on the wall, I peered around the corner. The breath flew from my lungs.

A woman stood several yards down the path, surrounded by that bluish light—definitely not the same light coming from the dingy yellow bulbs that hung from the ceiling. Her hair floated in wisps around her head, and she was smiling a tiny smile. I recognized her from the portrait in my blog post.

Sonja Hillebrandt.

Post: The Pirate Ghost of Crimptown
Comments: (6)
Anonymous: You poor, stupid girl. You have no idea what you're getting into.

PROOF. I'd said I needed proof to make me believe in ghosts, and here she was. But I still couldn't believe my eyes.

I stood, paralyzed, as Sonja drew closer. Weren't ghosts supposed to be transparent? Because she wasn't—she looked as solid as me. And her clothes were . . . wrong. No old-fashioned dress like in the photo. She wore a sweater, and . . . were those *jeans*?

Sonja stopped a few feet from me and held out her hand.

It was like being enveloped in a cloud of static electricity. All the hairs on my arms and neck stood straight up, and my skin tingled. I blinked furiously, my vision suddenly blurry. When something moved in my pocket, I nearly screamed before remembering the Elapse.

Tearing my eyes off Sonja, I pulled out the compact camera. It was turning off and on, off and on, the lens protruding and retracting. My hands shook as I flipped it on. *Proof.* A photo. I needed to get a photo of Sonja.

Her face swam before my eyes. My head felt fuzzy, like my brain had turned to cotton. I held the viewfinder up to my eye and took a deep breath.

It's dark, so you'll need a wide aperture. Hold it steady, Kat, steady—if the camera shakes even a little bit, the picture will blur . . . Kat? Are you listening to me? Kat!

"Leave me *alone*," I hissed. My mother's voice faded, and dimly, I realized another voice was yelling in the distance.

My eyes slid in and out of focus, but I could just make out movement behind Sonja. Someone was running straight toward us from the other end of the tunnel—yelling, panicked. Sonja reached for me again, her hand just inches away. Gripping the camera, I fumbled with the dials, trying to get her into focus. I zoomed in too far, and the locket around her neck filled the screen. *Locket? Locket. I've seen that locket before . . .*

"Stop moving," I whispered, dizziness causing me to sway. I had to get this photo. Actual proof.

Sonja's fingers closed gently around my wrist, and I gasped at the static spark. Her hand was warm, solid, real. When I pressed the button, the flash filled the tunnel like lightning.

Sonja stumbled—*ghosts stumble?*—and yanked my arm hard, pulling me into a cell. I tripped, too, and my head slammed into the wall just as the cell door clanked shut behind me.

Spots of light danced in my vision. I fumbled for my camera—Sonja was right there on the other side of the bars, I could still get the shot. I squinted at the screen, confused.

"What?" I mumbled, flipping the camera off and on. The message vanished, and I lifted the viewfinder to my eye. Through it, I saw Sonja on the other side of the bars. And next to her . . . a shape, an outline.

A boy.

Flash.

Sonja crumpled like a paper doll. Outline-boy made a motion as if to catch her, but his arms passed right through hers . . . except they didn't.

I lowered my camera just as Sonja's body hit the ground. But another outline—*her* outline—was still standing, gripping outline-boy's arms. Like her spirit had just stepped out of her body. Pain throbbed where I'd hit my head, and I squeezed my eyes closed for a second. When I opened them, the ghosts were gone.

But Sonja's body was still curled up on the ground.

Sam appeared and knelt next to her. "No, no, no . . . Are you okay? Can you hear me?" I realized he was the one who'd been yelling. I'd never heard Sam sound so panicked before.

"She fell," I mumbled, but Sam was patting Sonja's cheek and didn't notice me. A low buzzing filled my ears, and when I blinked, everything doubled before slowly sliding back together. I stayed there, slumped against the wall of the cell, as a distant herd of footsteps grew louder and louder.

Roland arrived next. Kneeling down, he felt Sonja's neck for a pulse, then checked her eyes. "She's breathing." Whipping the first-aid kit from his bag, Roland cast Sam an odd look. "Passed out. Did she get dizzy again?" he asked in a weirdly forced tone.

Sam nodded mutely. Roland's mouth was a thin line as he rummaged through the kit.

I almost giggled at the absurdity of the whole scene. *Ghosts don't get dizzy*, I told them, only I couldn't say it out loud. My mouth was too dry.

Jess nearly dropped her camera when she saw Sonja, her face ashen beneath her freckles. "Oh God, not again!" Turning, she shoved the camera at Mi Jin before dropping down on her knees next to Sonja. Dad appeared behind Mi Jin, out of breath. "Is that . . . ?"

Sonja, I told him. *Look, Dad. A real ghost! She fell down.*

Behind him, Jamie and Hailey came to a halt, staring as Roland held a small bottle under Sonja's nose. But Oscar shoved past everyone and crouched down next to her, his eyes wide with fear.

She fell, I told them. *Sonja fell*. But no one heard. I still couldn't seem to find my voice.

Sucking in a huge gasp, Sonja sat upright. But her face looked different; that wasn't Sonja's face . . .

"No . . ." I croaked, and Dad's head jerked up.

"Kat!"

He yanked open the cell door and knelt at my side, feeling my forehead. I brushed his hand away, hotly aware of everyone staring at me. "I'm fine," I said, although I felt anything but fine. "What about Sonja?"

Dad gazed at me, eyes filled with concern. "What, sweetie?"

"Sonja Hillebrandt." I struggled to stand, the fog

still clearing from my brain. "She fell. Is she . . . ?" I stopped, openmouthed.

Lidia stared up at me from where she sat on the floor, Roland's hand on her shoulder. Her eyes were glassy, her hair even frizzier than usual . . . but it was her. Lidia in her jeans and sweater, the locket around her neck. Next to her, Sam watched me intently.

"I thought . . ." I paused, closing my eyes. I'd seen Sonja, I was sure of it. But considering everyone was looking at me as if they feared for my sanity, I'd apparently been the only one. Except—

"Mi Jin," I said loudly, stepping out of the cell. "Hailey, what happened before you ended up in the cell? Did you see her?"

"See who?" Roland said, and Mi Jin frowned.

"I don't know what happened," she said. "I was filming Sam, and then I started feeling dizzy so I stepped away, and . . . and then I was in that cell with Hailey."

Hailey nodded. "I heard Sam and Lidia talking, and I was trying to find them to see who screamed, but the same thing happened. I felt woozy, and . . ." She rubbed her arms. "Crackly."

"Crackly?" Jamie repeated. But before Hailey could respond, the lightbulb overhead flickered.

For a few seconds, everyone stared at it apprehensively. Dad and Jess held their flashlights up, and Mi Jin lifted the camera. Then the flickering stopped, and the bulb stayed on.

Lidia slumped over, and Roland and Sam both reached for her. "It's fine, I'm fine . . ."

"Get her upstairs and get the front desk to call a doctor to check her out," Jess ordered Roland, who nodded as he helped Lidia to her feet. Jess turned to Dad. "Can you take Kat and Oscar to their rooms? I'll bring these two up and tell Thomas what's going on. Jack, Roland, Sam, Mi Jin—meet back down here in an hour."

"No, please let us stay!" Hailey cried. "We won't leave the cell, I swear!"

Jess shook her head, her face tense. "Sorry, kiddo. We don't want any of you to get hurt. I'm sure your dad will agree."

Hailey opened her mouth angrily, but Jamie put his hand on her arm and shook his head.

"I want the doctor to check Kat and Hailey out, too," Dad said tersely. "Mi Jin, as well. They were all pretty . . . out of it there for a minute."

"I just got dizzy, it's not a big deal," Hailey muttered, and my cheeks started to feel warm. At least she and Mi Jin hadn't thought they'd seen Sonja. Maybe I had a concussion or something.

Jess nodded in agreement. "I'll be in to check on Lidia as soon as I talk to Thomas," she added to Roland. Her face softened when she turned to Lidia. "Sure you're okay?"

Lidia smiled weakly, her eyes downcast. "Same old, same old. I'm fine."

Same old, same old? What, did she regularly turn into centuries-old dead women? But I kept my mouth shut. I was still light-headed, and the whole experience already seemed so distant and dreamlike . . . *Had* I really seen Sonja?

I tuned out the chatter as we all headed back up to the

theater. In the hotel lobby, I waved good-bye to Jamie and Hailey before Jess herded them off to their room, promising to bring the doctor around to each of us. As the elevator doors slid shut, I watched Roland ring the front desk bell impatiently while Sam guided Lidia to the sofa. "I'm fine, stop making a fuss," she said lightly. "You know how this goes, Sam . . ."

The elevator lurched, then started to rise. Dad stared straight ahead, a tiny muscle twitching in his cheek. I knew what that meant. Grandma called it his "patience timer." When that twitch started, it meant his patience had just about run out.

I swallowed. "Is Lidia really okay?" I asked Oscar, just to break the silence. He nodded, though he looked a bit shaken.

"Yeah. This happens sometimes."

"What is *this*, exactly?" I asked carefully. "I mean, what happened to her back there?"

He glanced at me. "Seizure. Wasn't it? You were there, not me. You saw her."

"Um . . . I guess, yeah."

The doors opened, and we followed Dad off the elevator. "I'm sure they'll be sending Lidia up soon," Dad said as Oscar swiped his key card. Oscar glanced at me, opened his mouth, closed it, and shut the door in my face.

"Well, good night to you, too," I muttered. Dad stayed silent until we reached our room. The door clicked closed behind him, and he turned to face me.

"Kat . . ."

"I'm sorry," I said immediately. "I know you said to stay there, but I—"

"Snuck off anyway," Dad interrupted. "Want to give me the short version of what happened?"

I swallowed hard. "I saw a light and . . . I guess I thought it might be Lidia or Sam. I wasn't going to go any farther than the end of the tunnel, I swear. But then I, um . . ." I couldn't say it. I just couldn't tell Dad I'd seen Sonja Hillebrandt. "I tripped and hit my head and fell into that cell," I finished lamely.

"Okay." Dad eyed me in a way that suggested he wasn't buying my story. "We're filming until five. You've got my cell number?"

"Yeah."

"We'll talk about this more tomorrow," Dad said. "And we'll come up with a set of new and improved ground rules that, if you're lucky, won't involve me hiring a bodyguard to shadow your every move."

I sighed. "Sure."

"Kat, look at me."

Steeling myself, I lifted my eyes to meet his.

"If this adventure of ours is going to work," Dad said, "I need to know I can trust you."

My throat suddenly felt hot, so I just nodded.

"Good night, Kat."

"'Night."

As soon as the door closed, I flopped back on my bed and stared at the ceiling. My eyes ached with exhaustion, but no way was I sleeping tonight. Not after I'd seen a ghost.

Or hallucinated that I'd seen a ghost. I wasn't sure which thought was more alarming.

Now that the fuzziness in my head had faded, I went over every detail in my mind. Lidia's sweater and jeans. Sonja's soft smile. Sonja's features were smaller, delicate. Lidia's were more angular, more defined. They didn't look alike. I'd seen Sonja clearly, zoomed in on her face, the locket around her neck—

Gasping, I shot up off the bed and jammed my hand in my pocket. The camera!

My fingers trembled as I flipped the Elapse on and started to scroll. There was Lidia's locket with the engraved *L*, and after that, the image of Sonja standing on the other side of the bars . . .

I held the camera close to my eyes in disbelief. The clarity wasn't great, but it was enough for me to see that the woman was definitely, absolutely, without a doubt Lidia.

Had I really somehow hallucinated Sonja? Was this all part of the "entertainment"? I had no idea how Lidia could have done all that, with the light and her floating hair and the static electricity . . . It was hard to imagine the crew pulling off that kind of hoax.

I stared at the photo for nearly a minute before I noticed what was next to Lidia. A sort of shape in the air next to her, a strange blur . . .

My heart pounded in my ears. It was faint, but unmistakable—and on a computer screen, it would be even more obvious.

The outline of a boy. I had a photo of a real, actual ghost.

Wasting no time, I grabbed Dad's laptop and plugged my camera in. Jess would bring the doctor up soon, but first I had a post to write.

Maybe Jamie and Hailey were right—with this photo, my blog could be the "something new" *P2P* needed to stay on the air.

CHAPTER THIRTEEN

THE THING 2: BACK FOR BLOOD

From: EdieM@mymail.net
To: acciopancakes@mymail.net
Subject: Phone call?

Hi, KitKat,
I miss your voice! How's everything? Want to chat tomorrow?
Don't worry about the time zone, you know I'm a night owl.
Love, Grandma

SUNLIGHT streamed through the window, heating my face until I sat up and threw the covers off. In the bed next to me, Dad was chainsaw-snoring away. I glanced at the clock—almost eleven. I wondered what time the crew had finally finished.

Twenty minutes and one hot shower later, I stood in front of Oscar and Lidia's door. Lifting my hand, I hesitated before knocking twice, very, very lightly.

"What are you doing?"

Startled, I swiveled around to see Oscar stepping off the elevator holding an armful of chip bags from the vending machines. "I, uh . . ." I felt flustered. Then I felt irritated for feeling flustered. "I wanted to see if Lidia was okay."

"She's sleeping right now." Oscar stopped in front of the door, but made no move to take out his key. "She has this heart condition."

I nodded. "Yeah, she told me."

"Every once in a while she has these . . . seizures. She has pills for it, but it still happens."

"Right." I pressed my lips together, thinking. After a few seconds, Oscar sat cross-legged on the floor and gave me an expectant look. Sighing, I slid down the wall next to him and stretched my legs out. My stomach growled loudly. Oscar held out a bag of chips.

"Thanks." I took it, eyeing him suspiciously. "Why are you being nice all of a sudden?"

"Because you look like you've seen a ghost," Oscar deadpanned, and I smiled despite myself.

"You have no idea."

"Sure I do." Oscar crammed several chips in his mouth. "Sonja."

I gaped at him. "Wait—you saw her, too?"

Swallowing, Oscar shook his head. "You said *Sonja.* Last night, when you were on the floor in the cell. Everyone heard you." He cleared his throat. "And I don't think *you* think Aunt Lidia had a seizure. So what happened?"

I ripped open my bag, debating how much to tell him. Really, I shouldn't have been confiding in him at all—we hadn't gotten along from the moment we met. But as much as I hated to admit it, Roland was right about us being alike. Oscar didn't believe in ghosts any more than I did. I had to tell someone what had really happened, and I wanted to tell someone who thought the same way I did.

I took a deep breath. "I saw her."

"Sonja?"

"Yeah." I stared at my chips. "She tried to put me in a cell, like she did with Mi Jin and Hailey. But when I took a picture of her, she, um . . . Look, I know this sounds insane, but one second she was Sonja and then she was Lidia."

"Does she look like Sonja in the picture?"

"Nope, she looks like Lidia," I admitted. "Right after I took the picture, Sonja sort of . . . um, stepped out of Lidia's body, and disappeared."

"Like she was possessed or something?"

"Yeah."

"Okay."

I glanced at him. "You don't believe me, right?"

Oscar chewed slowly. "I believe you think you saw Sonja," he said at last, and I almost laughed. That was exactly what I'd thought about Jamie and Hailey with the Ouija board. Pretty soon I'd be on my way to Planet Nutjob with half the fans in the forum.

"There's something else." I flicked a crumb off my shirt. "There was another ghost—the shape of a person next to her. A boy. You can see him in the photo."

"A *shape*?" Oscar repeated. "What do you mean?"

Standing, I brushed off my legs. "Come on, I'll show you."

Half a minute later, we stepped off the elevator and walked down the hall to room 301. Oscar had already pulled Lidia's key card from his pocket when I pointed ahead.

"Door's open. Someone's already in there."

"Can't you just get your dad's laptop?" Oscar asked.

"And risk waking him up?" I made a face. "I'm trying to put the lecture off for as long as possible, thanks. Maybe whoever's in there isn't using the laptop."

I pushed the door open a little, then all the way. The room was empty. Oscar and I glanced at each other, shrugged, and walked inside.

"Carlos? It's Roland."

At the sound of Roland's voice, my heart leaped into my throat. I shoved Oscar into the bathroom just as Roland stepped into view over by the closet, cell phone pressed against his ear.

"What's wrong with you?" Oscar hissed, and I flapped my hand at him to be quiet. I pushed the bathroom door closed, leaving it cracked so we could still hear Roland's conversation as he paced the room.

"Look, I know it's been a while, but I'm trying to get in touch with Emily and I was wondering if you . . ." There was a long pause, and Roland sighed. "I know, and I don't blame you. I tried to . . . No, I really did, and . . . Carlos, would you just stop for a second and . . . That wasn't how it . . . Okay, *listen*."

Oscar and I glanced at each other. Roland was just outside the bathroom door.

"It's going to happen again, Carlos." His voice was low and dangerous. "The *curse*, or whatever you want to call it . . . No, I'll take care of that, believe me. I just need to find Emily. Look, I know you're angry with me, but frankly, I don't care. I need you to—" He stopped abruptly, then muttered an impressive string of swear words. A few seconds later I saw him through the crack, slipping his phone into his pocket on his way past the bathroom. I waited until I heard the door click closed before exhaling.

"You," Oscar announced. "Are. Insane."

"Possibly," I agreed, stepping out of the bathroom. "Who cares, it was worth it. Now we know the truth about the stupid host curse."

"We do?"

I stared at Oscar in disbelief. "Weren't you listening? Roland told Carlos the curse was going to happen again! He said *I'll take care of that*. It really is just a publicity stunt." I shook my head. "And it sounded like he was trying to get Carlos to help him, even though he got him fired. No wonder Carlos hung up on—*ah!*"

The hotel door slammed into my arm. Rubbing my elbow, I spun around and found myself staring into Jamie's wide blue eyes.

"Sorry!" he said quickly. "Are you okay?"

"I'm fine," I replied in what was probably an overly casual voice. Jamie smiled and my anger dissipated. (Well, mostly. Oscar was still snickering at me.)

"What are you guys doing in here?" Jamie asked.

Oscar didn't miss a beat. "Spying on Roland because Ms. Conspiracy thinks he cursed the show."

"You think so, too," I shot back, irritated. "You heard what Roland said." Oscar shrugged and I checked the hallway before closing the door. "Where's Hailey?"

"No way she'll be up before noon," Jamie said. "She was

awake till almost five talking about your post."

It was a moment before I realized what he was talking about. "You read my post about Sonja already?" I asked, trying not to sound too flattered.

Jamie nodded. "Well, we figured you'd blog about it. Hailey kept refreshing the page until you posted. That picture is amazing."

"Yeah, that's what I wanted to show Oscar." I sat down behind the laptop, ignoring Oscar's loud, weary sigh. When I saw what was already on the screen, my mouth fell open.

P2P FAN FORUMS
Do you believe? Think again.

Anonymous
All you're watching is a bunch of morons hanging out in the dark faking sound effects. You've got a better chance of talking politics with a Chihuahua than Sam Sumners does of actually contacting a spirit.

Want proof? I've got it. Stay tuned to this thread to find out why this entire show is a sham.

skEllen [member]
OMG DO NOT TALK ABOUT SAM LIKE THAT HE IS PERFECT I MET HIM ONCE AND HE TOLD ME DOCTOR MEW DIDN'T BLAME ME FOR GETTING HIT BY THAT CAR SO HOW DO U EXPLAIN THAT????!!!!1!!!!11!!!!!!!!

Maytrix [admin]
Boys and girls, we've got ourselves a troll!

AntiSimon [member]
Who's Doctor Mew?

skEllen [member]
MY CAT. HE DIED LAST YEAR AND SAM CONTACTED HIM FOR ME.

YourCohortInCrime [member]
I'm listening, Anon. Enlighten me.

AntiSimon [member]
Don't feed the troll, YCIC. Sorry about your cat, Ellen.

"It's Roland," I whispered. "Anonymous is Roland. Look at the time—it was just posted an hour ago. He must've done it before we came in. And then he called Carlos."

"Carlos Ortiz?" Jamie asked, and Oscar filled him in on Roland's phone call.

I drummed my fingers on the desk. "The first time I met Roland, he admitted they fake stuff sometimes. He said, 'We do our best to make things entertaining.' Like the host curse."

Jamie frowned. "So you really think Roland actually fired all the other hosts?"

"I think he set them up, yeah," I said, relieved he was taking me seriously. "It started with Emily. She was in love with Sam, but Roland was in love with her. He was jealous—that's what my grandma says, anyway, and I think she's right. So he got her fired, and the ratings went up because everyone was wondering what happened to her. Then Carlos . . ." I paused, thinking. "Carlos was fired for writing that exposé about the show, but he denied writing it. And

125

he didn't—because *Roland* wrote it. He knew ratings would shoot up again if they lost another host."

"What about Bernice?" Jamie wondered. "They never explained why she left."

"Grandma said she was afraid of her own shadow," I said slowly. "That's why she only lasted four episodes. I asked Roland about her, too—he just said she got freaked out and left. He must have scared her off somehow. And now he's stirring things up in the forums because the show's probably going to get canceled after Halloween."

"But Roland asked Carlos if he knew where Emily was, remember?" Oscar said. "After he said he'd take care of the curse, he said, 'I just need to find Emily.' That doesn't make sense."

I gazed at the screen, dread settling like a rock in the pit of my stomach.

"Yes it does."

"It does?" Jamie glanced at the screen, too. "How?"

"The host curse," I said quietly. "My dad's next—two episodes, right? Then he's gone. But Fright TV wants to cancel the whole show after Halloween—two episodes from now. Unless something big happens." I swallowed. "Roland knows he can't keep doing the host curse. That's why he's looking for Emily. He wants to bring her back."

Oscar squinted at me. "What, to be the host again?" When I nodded, he laughed. "Why would that work? Most fans hate her!"

"Exactly!" I said. "They hate her, but they love gossiping about her. Haven't you seen those old threads in the forum?

She loved Sam, Sam was clueless, Roland was jealous . . . The fans love all the drama, you know?"

"That's true," Jamie admitted. "Although . . . if Roland's in love with Emily, why would he want to bring her back when Sam's still on the show?"

I frowned. "Maybe he thinks she's over Sam?"

"Maybe." Looking doubtful, Jamie grabbed the mouse and opened a new tab. "Oscar needs to see that photo of Lidia," he reminded me, and I leaned back as he typed in my blog's URL.

Lost in Crimptown
Comments: (27)

"Whoa, twenty-seven?" I made a move to click the comments open, but Oscar swatted my hand away.

"Hang on, I want to see the photo first."

"Fine." I scrolled down until the photo of Lidia filled the screen, and the three of us huddled close to the screen to study it. Maybe she didn't look like Sonja, but the image was still creepy—strands of hair floating around her head like she'd just pulled on a sweater straight out of the dryer, eyes wide and unfocused . . . and the outline of a boy at her side, reaching for her, just barely visible against the crumbling gray brick wall.

I glanced at Oscar. His mouth was open, but he closed it when he realized I was looking. "Okay," he said slowly. "That's . . . weird. What *is* it?"

"It's a ghost," Jamie said matter-of-factly. "Not Sonja, and not Red Leer—too small. The third ghost we contacted

127

with the Ouija board, remember?"

"Mi Jin said something about cameras picking up ghosts even when we can't see them," I added, tracing the outline with my finger. "Something about a broader spectrum of energy."

Jamie beamed at me. "So you really do believe now?"

Flushed, I pulled my hand away from the screen. "I'm not sure," I admitted. "I mean, I don't know how else to explain this picture. And . . . she was Sonja. Lidia *was* Sonja. She grabbed my arm, and it felt like . . . like electricity."

"So you think Sonja possessed her?" Jamie asked.

"I don't know what I think." I turned to Oscar. "Have you ever seen Lidia have a seizure?"

He shook his head, glancing back at the image of his aunt, glassy-eyed and wild. "No. But I never spent a whole lot of time with her before now—she was always traveling. And she and my dad aren't really close."

As soon as Oscar finished speaking, his face tightened. I stared at him, Sonja and Roland and the curse momentarily forgotten. This was the first time Oscar had even mentioned his father. Why wasn't he living with him?

Something about his expression told me not to ask.

Jamie cleared his throat. "It doesn't *look* like a seizure," he said, pointing to the screen. "I mean, don't people fall over when they have seizures? But you said she was walking down the tunnel, right, Kat?"

"Yeah."

"She *did* fall," Oscar said. "She was lying on the ground when we got there."

"Only after I took her picture," I pointed out. "But she was

128

walking before that. And she . . ." Sighing, I turned to face Oscar. "Look, her face was Sonja's face. I know you think I'm crazy, and I know it doesn't make sense, but that's what I saw."

Oscar gazed at the picture. "I don't think you're crazy."

"Kat?"

Startled, the three of us whirled around. Dad stood in the doorway, yawning.

"Hi," I said, suddenly nervous even though I wasn't doing anything wrong. "Everything okay?"

"Yup," Dad replied lightly. "Just need to talk to you about something for a few minutes."

He headed back into the hall without waiting for a response. Sighing, I stood up. "Time to get chewed out for running off last night."

Jamie made a face. "Good luck."

"Thanks." I glanced at Oscar, but his eyes were back on the picture of Lidia.

Dad was waiting for me by the elevator, hands stuffed in his pockets. I watched him press the up button. Worry lines creased around his bloodshot eyes. My stomach clenched uncomfortably. I waited until we were on the elevator, then blurted out:

"I'm really sorry again about last night. I didn't mean to—"

Blinking a few times, Dad waved his hand at me. "No, it's . . . not that. I mean, we still need to have that talk. But that's not why I came to get you."

The elevator doors slid open. Dad ruffled his hair absentmindedly as he stepped into the hallway. I followed him to our room, the knot in my stomach cinching tighter and tighter with each step. Something was up. Something really not good. Outside our door, Dad turned to face me.

"Your mother's on the phone."

The knot snapped.

A sort of floating numbness spread through my chest. I stood there silently, waiting. After a few seconds, Dad sighed. "Look, sweetie . . . I've really been trying not to push you. But it's been six months, and—"

"I don't want to talk to her."

"I know." Dad sounded so weary, I felt another stab of guilt. "And like I said, I've been trying to respect that. But this is different. She has . . . news."

News. A thousand possibilities jammed my brain all at once. *She got into a major art gallery. She finally opened a studio in Cincinnati. She scored a cover shoot for a magazine. She's moving to New York. She's moving to Paris.*

She wants to come back.

Not that I wanted her to. Not at all. But I wanted *her* to want to.

Dad swiped his key card and held the door open. I stepped inside, and he squeezed my shoulder.

"I'll be down in the breakfast room," he said before closing the door softly behind me. I listened to his footsteps fade as he walked down the hall, eyeing the phone on the desk. The light flashed red.

Steeling myself, I sat on the edge of my bed and picked up the receiver. "Hi."

A pause. Then: "Kat? Is that you?"

"Yeah." After half a year, I figured hearing my mother's voice again would be . . . I don't know. I thought it would make me *feel* something. But it didn't.

I heard her take a deep breath. "H-how are you?" she said.

"Okay."

"Good. That's good." Another pause. I stared at the wallpaper. Yellow with a swirly beige pattern. Fairly nauseating.

"Is it . . ." She paused, then there was the muffled sound of talking. I frowned. Did she have her hand over the mouthpiece? Who was she talking to? "Sorry, sorry," she said quickly. "So, Kat, what's it like in the Netherlands?"

"Fine."

"I'm so jealous of the traveling you're getting to do. Where are you headed next?"

"Belgium."

"Wow. And your grandma said something about a haunted prison next—sounds creepy!"

"Yeah." I twisted the phone cord around my finger and listened to her take a deep breath. *That's right, I'm not making this easy, huh? Poor you.*

"Well, um . . ." Mom cleared her throat. "So, I have some news."

News, news, news. I waited, tightening the cord until the tip of my finger went numb.

"I'm . . . engaged."

I watched the clock change from 12:06 to 12:07.

"Kat?"

"What?"

"I said I'm engaged."

My fingertip was starting to turn a sort of mottled dark purple. "What do you mean?"

"I . . ." She trailed off for a moment. "I mean, I'm getting married."

"That doesn't make sense," I heard myself say. My voice sounded calm. Detached. "You can't get married when you're already married."

Mom was quiet. In the background, I heard the theme music to some cartoon I'd forgotten the name of. "Well," she said at last. "Your dad and I are . . . taking care of that."

The cartoon sound effects got louder. Slowly, I began to realize what she meant. Married. Again. Second marriage. First marriage? Taking care of that. So:

Divorce.

Even though a small part of me had known this was probably going to happen, it was still sort of a shock. Not because I didn't think they'd ever really go through with it. But because I'd always figured when they did, Dad would be the one who told me. But he knew, about Mom's engagement— and Grandma, she probably knew, too—and neither of them had said anything. The list of people I trusted was shrinking even more.

"Kat? Are you still there?"

Releasing the cord, I flexed my numb finger until it started tingling. "Yeah, I'm here."

Mom sighed. Not in a sad way. In an irritated way. I'd heard that sigh a million times: when I wore my *Bride of*

Frankenstein T-shirt for school photos, when I polished off a pint of ice cream in one sitting, when I begged her to let me cut my hair short again and again and again . . .

"So. Congratulations." I gave each and every syllable equal, deliberate weight.

"Thank you," Mom replied. "We're thinking May for the wedding. I know it's sudden, but . . . well, that's how it happens sometimes. Anthony can't wait to meet you. I think you'll really like him, Kat. And I'd really love for you to be a bridesm—"

"You're staying in Cincinnati permanently, then?" I cut in. My face and neck suddenly felt hot, like I'd been sunburned by the hideous yellow wallpaper. It was peeling a little near the edge of the desk.

Mom cleared her throat. "No, Cincinnati . . . It didn't work out. I'm back in Chelsea."

I knew it. I *knew* it. "When did you get back?"

"June."

I froze in the act of picking at the frayed patch of wallpaper. "*June?*"

"Kat . . ."

"*June.*" I sat up, my pulse suddenly racing. "You left in *April.*"

"Kat—"

"You said you needed to move to the city for your *career,*" I said loudly. "You said you weren't happy in Chelsea. You said you wanted to be in galleries or open your own studio. *The next step.* That's what you said."

"Kat, I—"

"And you were only there for two months?" I laughed, a weird, high laugh that didn't sound like me. "And you—you didn't even bother telling us when you moved back. Are you seriously telling me you were in Chelsea all summer, and when I started school?"

"*Kat.*"

"What?" I yelled, squeezing the phone. "Why didn't you tell us?"

"You weren't taking my calls," Mom snapped. I felt a grim satisfaction at hearing her lose her patience. Not that it ever took much. "I told your grandmother, I told your father. They both thought I should be the one to tell you. But you didn't want to talk to me."

"I'm sorry, you're right," I said, interjecting as much sarcasm as possible into every syllable. "This is totally my fault."

"I didn't say that." Mom took a deep breath. "Look, I just . . . I wasn't happy in Cincinnati. I thought it's what I wanted, but it wasn't."

"So what *did* you want?"

Silence. I squeezed the cord again, listening to the cartoon in the background. Suddenly, I heard a child shriek in delight.

Wait, what was a kid doing with . . .

Oh.

I closed my eyes. "Who's that?"

Mom waited a beat too long to answer. "I'm sorry?"

"Who *is* that?" I repeated. "There's a kid there. Does your, um . . ." *Fiancé.* The word caught in my throat. "Whatever his name is, does he have a . . ."

"His name is Anthony." Mom paused. "And yes, he has a daughter."

For a split second, the room went blurry. It was like a physical shock—like seeing Sonja Hillebrandt gliding toward me down a dark tunnel. Then everything came into sharp, dizzying focus.

"She's five," Mom went on, her voice higher, nervous. "Elena. She's a sweetheart, you'd really like—"

"I've got to go," I said shortly. "Congratulations again."

And without waiting for a response, I slammed the phone down.

Forget ghosts. Now I had proof that the Thing was real.

CHAPTER FOURTEEN
THE DAWN OF DOCTOR PAIN

From: acciopancakes@mymail.net
To: EdieM@mymail.net
Subject: Re: Phone call?

Hi, Grandma,
Everything's great. Really busy, though. Maybe we can talk
next week.
Kat

I slept for five solid hours.

It was one of those dead-to-the-world sleeps, too. Facedown, arms tucked under the pillows, left leg hanging off the side of the bed. When I woke up, the comforter's stitch pattern was imprinted on my cheek.

I felt about as awesome as I looked.

After a scalding hot shower, I pulled on jeans and the *Attack of the Killer Tomatoes* T-shirt Grandma had given me for my last birthday. I rummaged through my bathroom-supplies travel bag and found a pack of rubber bands before giving my reflection a critical once-over. My hair was settling into the new cut, but it was still a little uneven—slightly shorter in the back than in the front. I gathered what I could up into a supershort ponytail that stuck out like a bristly makeup brush, then used a few barrettes to keep the stray pieces in place.

"Nice," I told my reflection. The Thing hovered in my peripheral vision, shaking its head disapprovingly. I turned my back on it and walked out of the bathroom.

When I stepped off the elevator and into the lobby, Hailey waved from the doorway as if she'd been waiting for hours.

"Kat!" she hollered. "We've been looking for you all day! Want to come get some dinner?"

"Sounds great!" My spirits lifted when I stepped outside and found Jamie standing near the entrance, studying his cell phone. He looked up and his face broke into a smile.

"Hey! I was wondering what happened to you," he said. "Everything okay with your dad?"

"Yup!" I said, maybe a little too cheerfully. "I ended up taking a nap."

"Your dad and Jess went to do a follow-up interview with the tour guide, and everyone else is editing and stuff. We were going to walk down the boardwalk and look for a pizza place Hailey swears she saw yesterday." Jamie glanced at my bare arms. "Do you want to get a jacket?"

"Nah, I'm good."

We set off down the boardwalk, the cold, salty wind whipping my face and arms. The ponytail and barrettes were a good call, I decided.

"Are you sure you're not cold?" Jamie asked again. I shook my head vigorously, spreading my arms out wide.

My T-shirt billowed around me like ship sails, and Hailey giggled. We talked about Crimptown for the rest of the walk, and by the time Hailey spotted the pizza place, I'd gone over the entire story about Lidia and Sonja in excruciating detail.

While we worked our way through an enormous pizza with ham and extra cheese, I outlined my theory about Roland for Hailey—that he'd fired Emily just because he was jealous that she was in love with Sam, but when the ratings spiked, he realized it was a great way to get publicity. So he set Carlos up by publishing that fake exposé in his name, then found some way to scare off Bernice.

"And now he's going to try to get rid of my dad and bring Emily back," I finished, dragging my crust across my plate to soak up the cheese grease. "He's delusional."

"Should we tell someone?" Hailey asked. "Our dad?"

"No," I said quickly. "Not yet, anyway. If your dad finds out what Roland's been doing, it might just make him want to cancel the show even more."

"What about Lidia?" Jamie suggested, and I frowned.

"Maybe . . ." I popped the last piece of crust into my mouth. "Let's ask Oscar first. Where is he, anyway?"

Jamie shrugged. "We played video games for a little while after you left, but he said he wasn't feeling good, so he went back to his room. Hopefully he didn't catch Lidia's cold."

"Oh." I chewed slowly, thinking. Lidia had definitely been looking ill since Crimptown. I pictured her crumpling to the ground, the ghost of Sonja stepping out of her body, helped by another ghost . . . a boy . . .

"Who do you guys think the third ghost was?" I blurted out. "The boy ghost in the photo?"

Hailey's eyes brightened and she sat up a little straighter. "I have a theory," she said seriously. "Sonja and Red Leer weren't the only ones who died during the fight, right? Other women died, and some of the prisoners, and some of Red Leer's men. I was thinking maybe . . ." Casting a glance around the near-empty pizza place, she lowered her voice. "I was thinking maybe it was her brother."

"Whose brother?"

"Sonja's!" she said eagerly. "Bastian Hillebrandt. Red Leer kidnapped him, right? He was one of the prisoners, and he was really young!"

"But I don't think he died in the tunnels," Jamie pointed out.

"Yeah, I'm pretty sure when Dad interviewed the tour guide he said Bastian survived thanks to his sister," I added.

"Aw." Hailey's face fell, and Jamie and I snickered. "Well, I mean I'm glad he wasn't killed," she added hastily. "I just really thought he was the ghost."

"The ghost reached out to catch her when she stumbled," I mused. "I don't think he was one of Red Leer's men. Maybe he was just one of the other prisoners who died."

"Hang on!" Hailey exclaimed. "Do you still have the paper I wrote all the Ouija messages on?"

"Yeah, I think so." I dug the paper out of my pocket, pushed the empty pizza tray to the side, and spread it out in the center of the table.

KEEP HER AWAY FROM THE MEDIUM
13 Xs
H E L L O
Is this Sonja?—YES
How many spirits?—3
G A T H E R T H E W O M E N
F R E E T H E M—NO
Is Sonja here?—NO
Who is this?—L E E R
Third ghost here?—YES/NO
F R E E T H—(Leer & ghost #3 fighting?)
K E E P H E R A W A Y F R O M T H E M E D I U M

"Look," Hailey breathed, tapping the bottom of the page. "After Sonja left and Red Leer was moving the planchette, the third ghost tried to take over. *Keep her away from the medium.*" She stared at me. "Whoever the third ghost is, he was with you in the theater. He gave you the same message there, too."

"So . . ." I chewed my lip. "You think maybe he's not a Crimptown ghost?"

Jamie shrugged. "He could be—the theater's got one of the entrances to Crimptown. Or he could be the show's ghost." He grinned at me. "Or maybe he's haunting *you.*"

"What?" I said, startled. The Thing leaned closer, and I shifted uncomfortably.

Hailey bounced a little in her seat. "Aw, maybe he's *your* ghost." She sighed dreamily. "Lucky you."

I stared at her, then burst out laughing. "You

guys are both totally insane."

"Wait a minute," Jamie said. "The camera—remember? You were with the crew when the camera started acting weird. *Thirteen* Xs. And that was on the boardwalk, far from the theater and way above Crimptown."

"He followed you!" Hailey placed her hand on her heart. "How romantic."

"Yeah, a ghost stalker," I said, trying and failing to keep a straight face. "That'd be very romantic and not at all creepy. So what do you think his thirteen Xs meant?"

Jamie opened his mouth, but Hailey cut him off, flapping her hands wildly. "Ohmigod, thirteen kisses! *Thirteen kisses!*"

I half-laughed, half-groaned. Jamie shook his head, his expression solemn. "It's the kiss of death, Kat."

"Thirteen of them." Hailey gave me a wicked grin, ducking when I threw my napkin at her.

"We should head back soon," Jamie said, glancing at the clock on the wall. "I told Dad we'd check in at eight."

Hailey snorted. "Yeah, like he'd notice if we didn't." I glanced at her in surprise as she slid out of the booth. "I'm gonna use the restroom first, okay?"

"Sure." Jamie watched her go, his brow slightly furrowed.

"What was that about?" I asked.

He blinked a few times. "What?"

"Hailey seems kind of . . ." I paused, unsure of how to say it. "Well, upset with your dad."

"Oh, yeah." Jamie wrinkled his nose. "It's no big deal. Our parents don't spend a lot of time with us, that's all. They're really busy at work," he added hastily. "I'm used to it, but

Hailey gets mad sometimes."

"Oh," I said. "What does your mom do?"

"Have you heard of *Head Turner*?"

Immediately, I pictured the stack of magazines that used to sit on our coffee table, each one featuring an impeccably dressed, flawlessly beautiful model on the cover. They disappeared sometime in July, although I'd never asked Dad what he did with them.

"Fashion magazine, right?" I asked lightly, and Jamie nodded.

"My mom's the editor in chief."

"Wow, that's really cool." I winced at how perky my voice suddenly sounded.

"She and Dad both travel a lot for their jobs," Jamie went on. "So, you know . . . We don't see them a lot. And even when they take us, like this trip, they just . . . They're always busy, so we still don't really see them much."

I made a face. "That sucks, I'm sorry."

"It's fine," Jamie said, a little too quickly. "Hailey's still upset that they missed open house at our school last month. They usually take turns with school stuff, but they got it mixed up this time. Dad thought Mom was going, Mom thought Dad was going . . ." He trailed off, shrugging. "Stuff like that's been happening more lately, that's all. Hailey can't stand it."

"It doesn't make you mad, too?" I couldn't help asking. "They're your parents. They're supposed to *be* there."

It came out louder than I intended. Pressing my lips together, I stared down at the table.

"Yeah, they are," Jamie agreed. "But . . . I don't know. Being angry about it isn't going to change things, is it?"

I didn't know how to respond to that. He was right, of course. But like Hailey, I had a hard time just letting go when something made me mad. The best I could do was pretend the problem didn't exist in the first place.

Hanging out with Jamie and Hailey turned out to be the perfect distraction from my phone call with She Who Must Not Be Named. We checked in with their dad when we got back to the hotel and found him on a call. He handed Jamie a handful of bills for the vending machines and waved us out of the room without lowering the phone from his ear. Hailey rolled her eyes but said nothing as we headed to see how the crew was doing.

Room 301 had been transformed into a makeshift production control room. Jess paced between the beds, barking questions and commands left and right. Lidia and Mi Jin kept scribbling, erasing, and scribbling again on this giant dry-erase board they'd propped up by the TV. Roland sat hunched over the laptop, reviewing footage and editing, a pile of sucker wrappers on the floor surrounding his chair. Next to him, Sam lounged in an armchair, occasionally interrupting Jess with comments like, "Sonja would prefer the first shot; it's more atmospheric."

"That was just lens flare," Jess said impatiently, and Roland snorted, choking a little on his sucker. I watched him closely, wondering if even now he was plotting his next anonymous post on the forums. Or if he'd managed to get in touch with Emily yet.

On Roland's screen, Sam and Lidia walked slowly through the tunnels. Lidia was rubbing her arms, like she had a chill. Roland rewound a few seconds and hit play again.

Sam tilted his head, watching the footage of himself. "That cold spot right there, that was where I felt Red Leer's presence most strongly," he mused. "Hopefully I can find it again when I go back down."

Jess sighed loudly. "Sam, we're not going back. We don't have time."

"Not to shoot," Sam said, his expression suddenly frustrated. "Sonja moved on, I'm sure of it—but Red Leer is still here. I might be able to help him."

Jess's lips were a thin line as she turned away from Sam. "Jack, did you find a few minutes we can trim out of the interview with the restaurant owner?"

"Yeah, I've marked a couple of places here . . ." Dad glanced up from a binder he was studying and noticed me hovering near the doorway with Jamie and Hailey. "Kat!" He hurried over, jumping aside as Lidia stepped back from the dry-erase board. I felt a sudden surge of panic at the concerned expression on his face. Was he was going to ask about the phone call in front of everyone?

"Hi, Dad!" I said in a pointedly cheerful voice. "How's the episode coming?"

Dad studied my face closely. I stared back without blinking. "All right," he said at last. "Good. Lots of material to work with."

"Even with you three getting in my shots," Jess added, wagging her finger at us. Her voice was light, but I heard a tinge of irritation in her tone and felt another rush of guilt.

Next to me, Hailey fidgeted. "Why *couldn't* you use those shots, though?" she blurted out. "I mean, if all of our parents gave permission, couldn't we be on the—"

"This isn't Nickelodeon," Roland yelled without taking his eyes off the screen.

"Hey, having kids on the show would probably help us bring in a younger audience," Jess joked, causing Roland to groan loudly.

Sam was watching me with a thoughtful expression. "That's not such a bad idea, actually. Children are often more receptive to messages from the spirit world," he said, and I shifted uncomfortably.

Shaking her head, Lidia stepped back from the dry-erase board. Her oversize lenses magnified the shadows under her eyes, and I couldn't help wondering if she should be working this hard after . . . whatever it was that happened to her last night. "Would you guys mind checking on Oscar?" she asked. "I think he's up in our room—I haven't heard from him in a while."

"Sure." As I turned to go, Dad put a hand on my shoulder, his raised eyebrows asking the question he didn't want to say out loud. I shrugged his hand off.

"You'd better get back to work," I said, smiling at him before turning and following Hailey and Jamie into the hall.

"They really *should* use the footage with us in it," Hailey muttered once the door was closed. "Especially you, Kat—

do you think Jess got there in time to film Sonja shoving you into the cell? I mean, can you *imagine* how much the fans would freak out if they saw that?"

"My blog post," I said suddenly. "There were a bunch of comments this morning, but I forgot to read them! Were they all people from the forums?"

"Mostly," Jamie replied, punching the button for the fourth floor. "They started a thread about it, too. They're pretty obsessed with the photo—you should check it out."

Oscar looked mildly surprised when he opened his door and found the three of us standing there. "Um, hi?"

"Lidia said to check on you." Hailey brushed past him without waiting for an invitation, and I struggled not to laugh.

"Can we come in?" Jamie asked loudly and pointedly, but Hailey was already sitting down at the desk and didn't seem to hear him.

Oscar shrugged and stepped aside. "Sure."

"Are you okay?" I squinted at him. His eyes were shiny and pinkish. "You look kind of . . ." I trailed off, reluctant to say it out loud. *Kind of like you've been crying.* "Tired."

"So do you," Oscar said, arching an eyebrow. "Are *you* okay?"

We stared at each other and for a moment, I felt like my mask had slipped. Oscar knew. Somehow, he knew about my mom's "news."

Then I shook it off. Just my imagination. It *had* to be. There was no way he could know.

The four of us spent almost an hour combing through

the comments on my Crimptown post, then the forum thread AntiSimon had started about the photo of Lidia. It was just like Roland predicted—a lot of them thought the outline of the boy ghost was faked (as if I knew how to edit photos like that). Some of them believed it was the show's ghost . . . or *wanted* to believe. But I could tell most of them were still just a little bit skeptical, even the really hard-core fans.

Not that I could blame them. I would be, too, if I hadn't seen it with my own eyes. And even so, a small part of me regretted being so honest. I'd published a post claiming to have seen the ghost of a woman killed hundreds of years ago, possessing Lidia until some random boy ghost helped her move on. Trish and Mark left comments that made it clear they thought I was joking—or at least, that they hoped so. (Grandma completely believed it, though. Shocking.)

While Oscar and Jamie raided the vending machines, Hailey and I flipped through the limited TV channels. Hardly anything was in English, so I hurried down the hall to my room to grab the *Invasion of the Flesh-Eating Rodents* DVD Grandma had given me. We'd just gotten to the extended shower scene (*not* nude—the shower curtain and careful camera work hid everything important, thank you) when Mi Jin stuck her head in.

"Just checking in on you guys . . ." Glancing at the screen, she squealed and let the door close behind her. "Edie Mills, oh my God! I love her!" Mi Jin sat on the edge of the bed where Hailey had sprawled out with a pile of candy bars. "*Flesh-Eating Rodents*—classic. *Vampires of New Jersey* is my favorite Edie movie, though. I was Maribel Mauls for Halloween a few years ago. Used a whole can of hairspray."

I wrinkled my nose. "*Vampires* is your favorite? Seriously? It's so cheesy!"

"That's why I love it!" Mi Jin leaned forward, squinting at the TV. "Hang on . . . I don't remember this scene! Are those guinea pigs?"

"Yeah, this is a special edition," I told her, holding up the case with *Never-Before-Seen Footage!* blazoned in red across the top, right above Grandma's wide, horror-filled eyes.

"Whoa, when did this come out?" Mi Jin grabbed the case and flipped it over to read the back. "I have *all* of her movies. She's the best."

"I don't think it's been officially released yet."

"Then how'd you get a copy?"

"My, um . . ." I closed my eyes briefly. *Good job, Kat.* "My grandma gave it to me."

Jamie shot me a curious look. "How'd she get it before it came out?"

"She's, uh . . . she's Edie Mills."

Four heads swiveled in my direction. "*What?*" Mi Jin yelped.

Oscar reached up from his spot on the floor and pressed a button on the laptop we'd connected to the television. On the screen, Grandma froze midscream, a rabid guinea pig gnawing at her neck. Everyone stared at me expectantly, and I sighed.

"Yeah, so, Edie Mills is my grandma."

"Um." Jamie squinted at me, then at the screen. "You and

your grandma kind of don't . . . look alike?"

"She's white," Hailey added bluntly, and I bit back a laugh.

"She's my mom's mom. I look more like my dad. Er, obviously."

"Oh, *wait!*" Hailey lunged for Oscar's laptop and sent the candy wrappers flying. "The comments on your blog—there's an Edie, right? There *is!*" She turned the laptop so we could see the screen, a triumphant smile on her face. "Edie M! She comments on every post! She's the one always asking for pictures of Sam!"

At that, Oscar burst out laughing. Mi Jin clapped both hands to her mouth, her eyes round with shock.

"Oh my *God*, Edie Mills is seriously your *grandmother*? Why didn't you tell us sooner?"

"Well, it's not like she's *that* famous," I said. "Most people have never seen her movies. I didn't know you had."

"Are you kidding? She's, like, my *idol!*" Mi Jin exclaimed. "No, for real—when I was in middle school, I only auditioned for the cheerleading squad because I wanted to be like Kimmy Kickwell in *Mutant Cheerleaders Attack*. They got mad when I brought fake blood to the first game to use during a routine, so I quit. And when I was sixteen, I was a cannibal clown for Halloween, and my friend Laura dressed up as Tina Soares—she even made this trapeze swing as part of her costume. And this one!" Mi Jin flapped her hand excitedly at the TV, where Grandma's battle with the guinea pigs was still paused. "*Vampires* was my favorite movie, but Katya Payne's definitely the best character Edie ever . . ."

Mi Jin trailed off. The room fell silent as realization dawned, and I sighed, bracing myself. Oscar was the first to say it.

"*Katya?*"

Giving him an innocent look, I ripped open another bag of Skittles and popped a few into my mouth. "Mmhmm?"

"Oh. My. God." Mi Ji gazed at me, shaking her head in disbelief. "You were named after Doctor Katya Payne, weren't you. Katya Sinclair."

Chewing slowly, I pretended to consider it. Then I shrugged. "Hey, it's better than Kimmy Kickwell."

"It's *awesome!*" yelled Hailey, while Oscar and Jamie cracked up. "No, shut up, you guys—she's named after a character her grandmother played in a horror movie. That is, like, the coolest thing *ever!*"

"Not just any character," Mi Jin added, her eyes still wide with awe. "Katya Payne—"

"Gets attacked by guinea pigs in the shower," Oscar cut in, and Jamie fell on his side, laughing. "Hiding any scars, Kat?"

Mi Jin swatted him on the head. "Stop, you don't understand—Doctor Payne is one of the best horror-movie heroines of all time. Edie won—"

"Doctor Pain?" Hailey interrupted, giggling. "Like, *ow* pain?"

"Oh man, I'm *so* calling you Doctor Pain from now on," Oscar said, grinning at me. I flicked a yellow Skittle at his forehead, sending Hailey into hysterics.

Jamie grabbed the laptop. "I'm changing the name of

your blog to *The Doctor Pain Files*," he announced, and a moment later a red Skittle bounced off his nose. Within seconds, the room was a tornado of flying candy, chips, and wrappers.

"I should get back downstairs," Mi Jin called, hurriedly backing up to the door. "You guys have a good night. Watch out for guinea pigs in the shower, Doctor Pain."

A half-empty bag of Cheetos smacked against the door the instant it closed behind her.

CHAPTER FIFTEEN
RETURN OF THE JERK

P2P WIKI
Entry: "Automatism"
[Last edited by Maytrix]

Automatism refers to a spontaneous, involuntary movement caused by spirits. In most cases, the individuals are unconscious of their actions, which are influenced by the presence of the spirit. Automatism may also be a sign of possession.

RING-*RING. RING-RING. RING-RING.*

"Make it stop," I moaned, blindly groping for a pillow and cramming it over my face. A moment later, I heard Dad flip the alarm clock off.

"Sorry about that." His voice was muffled, thanks to my pillow. "I must've hit snooze when I turned it off earlier."

"Mmmph."

"I'm heading downstairs to get some work done," Dad went on. "It's already after nine—try not to sleep in too much, okay?"

"Mmmph."

"Kat."

Heaving a sigh, I pulled the pillow off my face. "I'm on fall break, you know. We're not doing lessons this week."

"Yes, but you'll never adjust to the time-zone change this way," Dad said matter-of-factly. "Naps in the middle of the day, staying up late, sleeping in."

"Why bother getting used to it?" I mumbled. "We're leaving for Brussels in a few days, anyway."

"Brussels is in the same time zone as Rotterdam."

I wrinkled my nose. "Oh."

Dad headed to the door, then stopped and turned around. "Kat, about your phone call with . . ."

Rolling over to face the window, I yanked the blankets up and over my head. I heard Dad sigh, and a moment later the door clicked closed.

I slept for another two hours.

By the time I stepped off the elevator and into the lobby, it was almost eleven thirty. The breakfast room was empty except for Lidia and Oscar, who sat at a table in the corner talking quietly. I studied the remains of the free continental breakfast: a few cantaloupe slices, some sugar-free, taste-free bran cereal, and two muffins I was pretty sure were from yesterday.

Okay, maybe Dad was right. I needed to start waking up earlier.

Grabbing both muffins and a couple of grapes I found hiding beneath the cantaloupe, I headed over to Oscar and Lidia. "I'd kill for some bacon pancakes," I announced, pulling out a chair. They jumped, startled, and I set my plate down. "Sorry, I thought you saw me come in."

"No, we were just . . ." Blinking, Lidia smiled a little too cheerfully. "Just chatting. How'd you sleep?"

I shrugged. "Okay. How's the episode coming?"

"Great!" Lidia chirped. "Jess didn't want to use the footage of my seizure, but I convinced her." She paused, toying with the locket around her neck. "So . . . we all read your blog post last night."

"You did?" I glanced at Oscar, but he was staring blankly at his uneaten toast. "Wait, who's *we*?"

"Everyone," Lidia said. "Jess, Roland, Sam, Mi Jin. Thomas Cooper. And your dad, of course. That, um . . ." She squeezed her eyes closed for a second, as if she had a headache. "That photo of me was certainly interesting."

I choked a little on a grape. "I should've asked," I said, suddenly mortified. "I shouldn't have just posted that without asking you first. I'm really sorry."

Lidia waved dismissively. "No apologies necessary. But . . ." She coughed, and I flinched at how raspy it sounded. "But now that your blog is getting attention from fans of the show, we're going to have to monitor it. Make sure you don't publish anything . . . er, inappropriate."

"Inappropriate? Like what?"

"Anything that could violate someone's privacy, for example," Lidia said. "I'll be honest, Kat—I think it's great that you're blogging about the show. The fans seem to love it. But not everyone feels the same."

"Who was upset about it?" I asked, then answered my own question. "Roland."

Nodding, Lidia took a sip of coffee. "He's pretty against having any sort of behind-the-scenes blog, especially one written by a kid. Jess felt the same. But I convinced them that the most important thing is how much the fans love it. In the end, they agreed with me . . . so long as you allow us to check your posts before you publish them, and make any changes we ask. We'll need to monitor the comments, too—you've had some odd ones pop up."

I sat back in my chair, chewing my lip. I hadn't been planning to post about Roland and the host curse—not yet, not without proof. Still, the idea that I couldn't post *anything* without his approval was irritating. I glanced at Oscar again, but he refused to look up, which just increased my annoyance. What was his deal this morning?

"Kat, it's your blog," Lidia said. "If you want to keep writing whatever you like without us monitoring, you can set your blog to private and just give your friends and family access. But if your blog is going to be part of the show, then we have to treat it that way. We don't air any footage without approval from everyone on the crew. Same applies to a behind-the-scenes blog."

I swallowed. As much as I hated to admit it, that was fair. "Okay," I said. "I'll show you my posts before I publish them."

"Thank you." She was still twirling the necklace around her fingers. "So . . . you really thought I was Sonja, huh?"

I nodded, my mouth full of stale blueberry muffin.

"I've been trying so hard to remember what happened, but . . ." Trailing off, Lidia sighed. Then she smiled at me. "Starting to believe, are you?"

"Er . . . I guess I'm keeping an open mind." I hesitated,

watching as Lidia twisted the necklace tighter and tighter around her trembling fingers. Her face was flushed, her eyes shiny. "Lidia, are you feeling okay?"

"Hmm?" Lidia blinked a few times, her hand falling still. "Oh, I'm still just trying to kick this cold. Nothing to worry about." Yawning, she pushed her chair back and stretched. "All right, back to work. I think the others are in the conference room."

She touched Oscar's arm lightly, but he didn't look up. For a brief second, a strangely familiar expression flickered across Lidia's face. She'd left the breakfast room before I realized where I'd seen that look before.

It was exactly how Dad looked at me this morning when he'd tried to ask about my phone call with Mom and I ignored him.

I crammed the last of the muffin into my mouth, eyeing Oscar. "We saw an arcade on the boardwalk yesterday," I said at last. Oscar lifted a shoulder, still staring at his toast. "Want to go check it out?" Another shrug. I hesitated, then pressed forward. "I was thinking we could find Jamie and Hailey and—"

"No, thanks," Oscar said shortly. Tossing his napkin on the table, he got to his feet. "See you later." And with that, he walked back out into the lobby.

I stared after him, mouth open. I hated to admit it, but him blowing me off kind of hurt my feelings. Although on second thought what did I expect? Oscar had been a jerk since we'd first met. Just because he'd acted like a seminormal human being last night when we were all watching movies didn't make him a nice guy all of a sudden.

Beep! Beep! Beep!

Frowning, I pushed aside the pile of napkins in the middle of the table. A smartphone's screen was lit up with a message. Alarm: TAKE YOUR MEDS!

Lidia's reminder about her heart medicine. I stood quickly, swiping the alarm off.

I was halfway to the conference room before I realized that the phone was still lit up. The alarm message had disappeared, leaving the screen open to whatever Lidia had been reading earlier. I was about to close it when Oscar's name caught my eye.

Dear Ms. Bettencourt,

In regard to your brother, Oscar Bettencourt Sr., and his request for parole: After careful review during yesterday's hearing, we regret to inform you parole has been denied. We will notify you when the date for his next annual hearing has been set.

Sincerely,

Grace Fletcher

Lafferty Federal Correctional Institution

For a few seconds, I just stared at the screen. Then guilt flooded through me as I realized I was reading what was obviously a very private e-mail. I pressed the button on the smartphone, and the screen went black. But I could still see the words in my mind, and with a slow, dawning horror, I realized what they meant.

Oscar's father was in prison. And he apparently wasn't getting out anytime soon.

Still staring at the screen, I walked around the corner and ran straight into Sam.

"Oh, sorry!" My voice was all high and weird. But Sam seemed preoccupied, as usual.

"Have you seen Lidia?" he asked, glancing around the lobby.

I tried to sound casual. "Conference room. She left her phone at breakfast. I was just bringing it to her."

Sam faced me, his blue gaze suddenly intense. "You thought she was Sonja."

My mouth went dry. "Oh . . . You saw my blog post?"

"Post?" Sam frowned. "Oh, yes—Lidia showed us. But when we were in the tunnels, you called her *Sonja*."

"Yeah, but—"

"You weren't hallucinating."

I stared at Sam silently for a moment. "How do you know?" I whispered.

"People always doubt their first paranormal experience . . . and second, and third," he said. "You think if you tell someone, they'll think you're crazy, so you convince yourself it was a trick of the light, or a concussion, or some other excuse. When you start to doubt—that's the real trick. You convince yourself of some other explanation. You trick yourself out of believing. But your eyes didn't lie."

I just stood there, unable to look away. For the first time, I really, truly understood why people loved Sam Sumners, and it had nothing to do with his looks. His expression was open and earnest, and his airy, flaky demeanor had vanished—he spoke with such conviction, I found myself nodding along.

"I believe you, Kat," Sam said simply. "You saw Sonja. You saw her leave Lidia's body."

Swallowing hard, I nodded again. "That other ghost helped her," I said. "The one in the photo. A boy, I think."

Sam's lips curved up in a small smile. "Yes, him. He likes you, I think."

"What?" I felt my face heat up. "Who is he?"

"A friend of the show." Sam laughed when I rolled my eyes. "No, really. He's always with us. But I've never been able to communicate with him—he doesn't like me." He paused, looking thoughtful. "Ghost children always prefer other children to adults, though. They trust other children. That's why he's been reaching out to you."

"He tried on my first day in Rotterdam." I couldn't believe I was saying this out loud. But something about Sam made me want to talk about it. "When I used the laptop, there was a blank document open, but it printed out with a message: *Keep her away from the medium.*"

Sam sighed deeply, his eyes glazing over. "Ah."

"Do you know what it means?" I asked hesitantly.

After a moment, Sam nodded. "Yes. I think I might."

I waited, then cleared my throat. "Well? Who does he want you to stay away from?"

Down the hall, the doors to the conference room opened. Dad and Jess exited first, laughing and chatting. Roland, Lidia, and Mi Jin followed, all carrying armfuls of folders and binders. They headed down the hall toward the back exit. Glancing over his shoulder, Roland saw Sam and me.

"We're going back to that café Jess found," he called to Sam. "Coming?" His eyes flickered to me, and I stared back defiantly.

"I'll be right there," Sam replied. I waited until Roland had turned back around before touching Sam's arm.

"Who does he want you to stay away from?" I repeated. Sam blinked, his gaze sliding back over to the rest of the crew.

"It doesn't matter," he said quietly. "I'm already trying to keep my distance."

He gave me a small smile before wandering down the hall after the others. It was only after the exit doors closed behind them that I remembered Lidia's phone was still in my hand.

CHAPTER SIXTEEN

THE SECRET OF THE DEAD AIR

Post: The Eternal Prison

The day after tomorrow, we're heading to Brussels to visit Daems Penitentiary, which is a few miles (er, kilometers) outside the city. Out in the middle of nowhere, according to Dad. He's been doing lots of research to prepare for his interviews, and the prison has a history pretty much as creepy as Crimptown. In 1912, there was a massive escape attempt that ended really gruesomely.

It started with one prisoner, who managed to steal a key from a guard during lunch. That night, he unlocked his door and quietly crept from cell to cell. He told each prisoner to wait until midnight, then all break out of their cells at the same time. That way, the guards would be overwhelmed and more of them would be able to escape. He promised he'd hide in the tower and deactivate the electric fence that surrounded the courtyard. The prisoners all agreed to his plan. So the first prisoner unlocked all the cells, but left their doors closed. Then he crept up to the tower, and everyone waited.

At midnight, chaos erupted. The prisoners all burst out of their cells and started running out into the courtyard for the fence. The first prisoner threw the switch and turned the fence off, then hurried downstairs to make his escape.

A few prisoners were killed, but some guards were, too. There weren't enough guards left to stop most of the prisoners from escaping. All around the courtyard, men were climbing the fence.

They were almost free.

But one guard had noticed the first prisoner fleeing the tower, and realized he'd deactivated the fence. So the guard ran up the tower and flipped the switch back on.

Ninety-four men were electrocuted. They fell from the fence, dead before they hit the ground.

The prison was abandoned after that. Dad said people are so superstitious about it that after the bodies were taken away, the city could never get anyone to buy the property, or even set foot on it to clean it up. The local legend is that every night at midnight, the ghosts of those ninety-four men roam the courtyard and try to escape. But they never make it past the fence. Locals call it *la Prison Éternelle*—the Eternal Prison.

JAMIE finished reading my post out loud and sat back in his chair.

"Wicked," Hailey announced, and I grinned.

"Yeah?"

She nodded, still studying the pictures on the screen. "Yeah."

"It's great," Jamie agreed. "These photos are really cool, too."

"Jess found those for me," I told him. Jess and Dad had read my post last night before I'd published it. After what Lidia had told me, I'd kind of expected Jess to be annoyed by the whole thing. But she'd actually seemed impressed. She'd even said my blog reminded her of an article Dad had written for their college newspaper about local urban legends.

Hailey sighed. "This episode is going to be so creepy. I wish we could come."

"Me too," I said, and I meant it. I'd barely known the Coopers for a week, but I was really going to miss them. Especially with Oscar being so . . .

Well, antisocial would be the nicest way to put it. Not that I blamed him one bit.

I hadn't told Oscar what I'd learned about his father. I felt awful about invading his and Lidia's privacy, even though it was by accident. And every time someone said *prison* or *prisoner*—which was, like, a hundred times a day, since they were all preparing for the next episode—I cringed.

Oscar never flinched. But then, he'd been spending a pretty decent amount of time holed up in his hotel room. Except for yesterday, when, after a lengthy video chat with Trish and Mark, I'd found Oscar in Mi Jin's room, where they'd been paired up against Jamie and Hailey in what was apparently a pretty epic *Mario Kart* battle. Oscar had been laughing and everything, but his eyes had still looked funny. Pink and a little too dry, like he'd been holding back tears for so long, he didn't even have to try anymore.

"Hell*ooo?*"

Blinking, I realized Hailey was waving her phone in front of my face. "Sorry, what?"

"Laser tag!" she said excitedly. "That giant arcade we saw the other day on the waterfront has it. Dad just texted—he said he'll be ready to leave in fifteen minutes. You're still coming, right?"

I smiled. "Yeah. Is, um . . . is Oscar coming, too?"

"We told him about it yesterday," Jamie replied, standing up and stretching his arms. "I think he's in his room—I'll see if he still wants to go."

After Jamie left, I clicked over to the *P2P* forums to see if there were any more comments about the picture of Lidia. But the most recent thread update pushed all thoughts of the photo from my mind.

P2P FAN FORUMS
Do you believe? Think again.

Anonymous
I said I'd prove this show is a fraud, so here we go. *P2P* claims to be the most haunted show on television, starting back with the dead air during its first episode. What really happened in the lighthouse? As it turns out, it was just a botched attempt at tricking hapless viewers. Don't believe me? Watch this little clip and see for yourself . . .

"It's the same one," I breathed, clicking the link to the video. "I bet it's the same one . . ."

"The same one as what?" Hailey asked eagerly, but the video was already playing.

And sure enough, there were Sam, Lidia, and Emily seated around the same small table, holding hands, the single dim bulb dangling over their heads. Lidia shivered with anticipation, while Sam looked perfectly peaceful. Emily gazed at Sam in a worshipful way that hovered between laughable and creepy.

Hailey let out a low hiss. "This is the one you were talking about. The video that randomly started playing, then all the lights went out, right?"

"Yeah." I glanced around my room. It was hard to feel creeped out with all the sunshine streaming in through the windows, but my arms and neck still prickled. "This is the scene . . . but it's not the same video. Look."

I pointed at the screen. A camera set up on a tripod in front of the table was just barely in the shot, capturing the video I'd seen. This camera sat at an odd, high angle, almost like it was hidden. And the quality wasn't nearly as good for the video or audio. In fact, I was pretty sure it had been taken with a phone.

"Close your eyes," Sam said softly.

"Are you sensing a presence?" Emily whispered loudly, her gaze still locked on Sam.

Hailey snorted. "I can't stand her. Bernice was the best host. I mean," she added quickly, "besides your dad."

I smiled without taking my eyes off the screen. "His first episode hasn't even aired yet."

"Well, that's true."

The lightbulb flickered and I leaned forward. "Here we go. Watch this . . ."

Emily wiggled in her chair. *"Sam, I think—"*

Lidia's eyes flew open . . . and she stared right into the hidden camera. Right at us.

Goose bumps broke out on my arms. Hailey gasped, recoiling a little. The lightbulb exploded, plunging the scene into darkness, and Emily shrieked. Shadows moved across the screen as Sam and Emily bumped into one another, knocking over chairs. Behind them, the door flew open. Light from the hallway filled the small room, and Roland stood framed in the doorway.

"Oh no, poor Lidia," Hailey murmured, and I shook my head in disbelief. Lidia was sprawled facedown on the table, completely unconscious. Sam reached for her, but Roland beat him to it.

"Jess, hurry!" he yelled over his shoulder. *"Lidia? Lidia, can you hear me?"* Gently, Roland rolled her back into her chair, her glasses hanging askew. He took them off and placed them on the table, checking Lidia's pulse with his other hand. Her eyelids fluttered open, and she sucked in a deep breath.

"Wha? 'Mokay," she murmured. Roland's shoulders slumped in relief, and Sam sank back down in his chair, looking shell-shocked. Emily stared at Lidia with a mixture of fear and irritation.

"What's wrong with her?" she snapped. *"And what was that? Did you use one of those trick lightbulbs Jess bought?"*

Roland didn't look up. *"She fainted,"* he said, jaw clenched. *"Turn the camera off."*

Glancing around the room, Emily headed over to the camera on the tripod and flipped it off. A few seconds later, the video clip ended abruptly.

Hailey exhaled loudly. "Oh boy," she said, clasping her hands over her head. "Trick lightbulbs?"

I grimaced, clicking back over to Anonymous's post.

Whoops! Looks like they let a little secret slip there. Fake bulbs. For shame. Lidia puts on quite a performance, too. No wonder they ditched this footage and went for the dead air scam instead.

It's all just a hoax, folks . . . more soon . . .

YourCohortInCrime [member]
Well, there you go. Thanks for the proof, Anon. Disappointing, but not surprising.

spicychai [member]
i am devastated

AntiSimon [member]
Hang on—Anon, how'd you get this video?

YourCohortInCrime [member]
Does it matter? The show's a fake.

skEllen [member]
OMGOMGOMGOMGADFIOAWENG NOOOOOOOOO!!!! ROLAND WOULD NEVER SCREW UP SAM'S SEANCE LIKE THAT!!!!! EMILY IS EVILLLLLLLLLL!!!!!!!!111!!!!!!!!11!!!!!!!1

Anonymous
Emily Rosinski was the best thing about this sorry show. She can do a lot better than Sam, believe me.

AntiSimon [member]
EMILY was the best thing about this show? Uh . . . do you even WATCH this show, Anon?

Maytrix [admin]
Okay, everybody calm down. All that video proves is that the exploding bulb *might* be fake. (Yes, MIGHT. Roland doesn't confirm it.) And even if they've used fake bulbs, that doesn't mean *everything* is faked. Also, I'm not convinced Lidia was acting. Remember Kat Sinclair's recent blog post? Lidia passed out in Crimptown, and Kat's right about her heart problems. Lidia's

mentioned that on the show before. She looked like she had some sort of seizure in this video, too.

Simon's question is a good one. Anon, we welcome everyone on this forum, skeptics and believers alike, so long as the conversation stays respectful. Please register to be a member— you don't have to publicly reveal any information about yourself. You and I can chat privately about your sources.

beautifulgollum [moderator]
Maytrix has a great point. The lightbulb thing is a bummer, but it doesn't mean the whole show's a fake.

YourCohortInCrime [member]
Your problem is you want to believe.

AntiSimon [member]
Your problem is you don't.

skEllen [member]
THIS IS THE WORST DAY OF MY LIFE

"It's Roland," I said grimly. "I *knew* it was Roland."

Hailey chewed her lip. "Yeah, it has to be someone from the show. Nobody else would have that video. It looked like that camera was hidden."

"And Roland was on the forums the other day, right when Anonymous first posted," I added, pointing to the screen. "And look at what he said here. *Emily Rosinski was the best thing about this sorry show. She can do a lot better than Sam.*" I snorted. "Grandma was right—Roland's jealous. And delusional. I bet he thinks if he gets her back on the show, she'll fall in love with him instead."

168

"So what do we do?" Hailey asked. "Tell Lidia? Or my dad?"

I was already heading for the door. "We can't tell anyone yet. Not without proof."

I put all my anger and frustration about Roland into three solid hours of laser tag, scoring ten hits in the first fifteen minutes. I'd never played before, but it was pretty similar to paintball, which I loved. Despite my mother's protests, my thirteenth birthday party had been at this huge outdoor paintball field just outside of Chelsea. I came home with a medal, but all she cared about was my new tennis shoes, all spattered with mud and paint.

Oscar's mood seemed slightly improved, so I filled him in on Roland's latest anonymous post in the forums as we crouched behind a short wall to catch our breath.

"So you want to spy on Roland again?" Oscar said.

"Not *spy*," I said impatiently, leaning around the side of the wall and aiming my laser gun at a teenage girl with dark blond hair. "Just . . . keep an eye on him. Find some way to prove he's going to do something to get rid of my dad so he can bring back Emily." I took my shot, and a second later the top right shoulder of her vest glowed red.

"And that's not spying?"

I rolled my eyes. "Look, you don't have to help. It's my dad who's about to get fired, not . . ." I trailed off, mortified at what I'd almost said. *Not yours.*

I was saved from having to think of something else to say when Oscar's vest lit up blue.

We glanced up just as Jamie threw himself behind a glowing green column. We took off after him, weaving between columns and around other players. Finally, Jamie spun around to face us, his back pressed against the side of a fluorescent-pink staircase—but before any of us could fire, the center of Oscar's vest lit up red.

"What the . . . Who did that?"

"Gotcha."

The three of us looked up to see Hailey, lying on her stomach on the top step with her laser gun aimed right at Oscar, smiling smugly. With an exaggerated wail, Oscar staggered around in circles, clutching his chest. He fell to the floor, limbs twitching. Between his melodramatic howls of pain and Hailey's contagious laughter, for a few minutes I managed to forget the Thing had been breathing down my neck all afternoon.

Post: The Eternal Prison
Comments: (1)
Anonymous: Nice post. Enjoy your last episode.

SAYING good-bye to the Coopers was painful.

"We'll e-mail lots," Hailey promised. "And we can video chat!"

"Promise?" I asked, and she nodded vigorously.

We were sitting on the couch in the lobby, waiting while their dad checked out of their room. Jamie pulled his laptop out of his backpack and flipped it open. "Almost forgot to show you this!" A second later, he turned so the rest of us could see the screen, and Oscar started laughing.

THE DOCTOR PAIN FILES
A behind-the-scenes look at the most haunted show on television.

"How did you do that?" I cried in amazement. It was my blog, but way cooler-looking. Jamie hadn't just changed the title—the whole look was different. The background was a world map, the countries a shade of gray barely lighter than the charcoal water. The header stretched across the top looked like a blurred image of a tunnel filled with a bluish light surrounding the warped black outline of a person in the center. A wispy, animated fog drifted around the title.

"It's only a template," Jamie said quickly. "And I just used Doctor Pain as a joke—I made another version with your real name. You'd have to log into your blog to upload it. If you want it, I mean."

"Um, yes, please." I leaned closer, watching the fog twist around each letter. "This is amazing. You're really talented."

Jamie's cheeks reddened. "Thanks. You have to keep posting, okay? See if you can get more photos, especially."

My fingers twitched at the thought of the Elapse. "I will, but I doubt it'll do any good," I said. "Roland's going to do something to get my dad fired, I know it. I showed you that anonymous comment he left on my last post. *Enjoy your last episode.*" I tried to sound dismissive, although in truth that comment had creeped me out a little. I'd deleted it before Dad or anyone else on the crew could see.

"That's why you have to keep posting." Jamie lowered his voice, glancing at his dad. "The fans love the curse. But they love your blog, too. And if your dad leaves, then you leave, and the blog's finished. Don't you think they'd rather have all this cool behind-the-scenes stuff than just seeing another host get canned?"

He had a point. My post about Crimptown had gotten almost seven hundred hits, mostly thanks to that photo of Lidia. Maybe my blog actually could be the "something new"

Fright TV thought the show needed to bring in more fans.

Hailey groaned, pointing at the doors. Through the glass, I saw a taxi pull up to the curb.

"Ready, kids?" Mr. Cooper called. Jamie closed his laptop and zipped his bag closed.

"Coming!" We all stood, Hailey and Jamie gathering up their bags. Hailey hugged me, then Oscar.

"Promise to tell us all about the prison!" she insisted as we walked to the doors. "Oh, and try the Ouija board again there! Oh, oh, and tell us if your stalker ghost gives you any more messages!"

"I will," I said, smiling. But a heavy sadness filled me as I watched her and Jamie pile into the taxi. It had been nice having friends here while everyone else was working. They waved through the back window, and I waved back until the car disappeared around the corner.

For a few seconds, Oscar and I just stood there in silence. That was the other thing about the Coopers—Oscar and I almost got along with them here as buffers. We hadn't technically had an argument in a few days. But things between us were still . . . prickly. It didn't help that I felt a rush of guilt when I remembered the e-mail about his father. I had to tell him I knew.

Oscar shoved his hands in his pockets. "What time did Jess say we're leaving?"

"Five, I think," I replied. "Hey, Oscar?"

"Yeah?"

"Are you, um . . .?" I paused, wishing I'd thought this through better. "I was—"

"Oscar!"

We turned to see Lidia in the entrance, her frizzy hair pulled back into a bun. She gave Oscar a bemused sort of smile.

"I thought you were going to pack this morning, but apparently you decided to fling your belongings all over our room instead." Her voice was even more hoarse than it had been yesterday.

Oscar rolled his eyes. "It's not *that* messy."

"Come on, you know it's going to take you forever to get packed." Shrugging, Oscar headed inside. Lidia gave me a pointed look. "Are *you* packed?"

"No," I admitted, following Oscar.

Lidia sighed. "Two peas in a pod, I swear."

Oscar and I glanced at each other briefly before looking away. I followed them to the elevator, saying a silent prayer of thanks that Mi Jin hadn't been around to hear that.

At six thirty that evening, I was curled up in the back of an old prison van. Jess had bought it that morning, saying she could sell it once we were finished in Brussels, so it was cheaper than renting a regular van. The seats weren't exactly comfortable, but at least it was roomy. A sliding door separated the front half from the back. Jess insisted on timing our drive so that we would drive into Brussels at sunset, which was right now. So while the rest of the crew was crammed into the front getting footage of the drive into the city and talking about the haunted prison, Oscar and I lounged in the back reading Mi Jin's comic books. Dad's voice was just audible through the door as he summarized the tragic Daems Penitentiary story. "Nearly one hundred men died during the escape attempt, most of them on the electric fence . . ."

Finally, I tossed my *Avengers* comic down. "Oscar, I should tell you that I know about your dad."

His head jerked up, his eyes wide. "You what?"

"I know about your dad," I repeated. "That he's . . . you know, in prison. Lidia left her phone on the table the other day and her alarm went off to remind her to take her heart medicine. When I turned it off, I saw an e-mail about his parole getting denied. It was an accident, and I'm sorry. But I saw it."

Slowly, Oscar lowered *X-Men*, blinking a few times. "Oh."

"I'm really sorry," I said again. "Not just that I saw it, but because . . . well. That really sucks."

He shrugged. "It's okay."

"Do you, um . . . ?" I hesitated, and Oscar watched me warily. "Do you want to . . . to talk about it, or anything?"

After a second, the corner of his mouth lifted. "Talk about it? Why?"

I sighed in frustration. "I don't know, I'm just trying to help."

"How will talking about it help?"

"You know what? Never mind." Grabbing the comic, I opened it up and furiously flipped through the pages to find my spot. "I was just trying to be nice."

We were silent for nearly a minute, listening to Jess and Roland argue about the directions. Then Oscar said: "Do you want to talk about your mom getting married again?"

The van hit a bump, and I gasped as *Avengers* went flying out of my hands. *"What?"*

Oscar rubbed the back of his head where it had bumped into the side of the van. "If talking about stuff is so helpful, why don't you talk about your mom getting engaged?"

"How do you know about that?" I demanded, sitting up straight.

Sighing, Oscar tossed his comic down. "When I first got here, I kept waking up really early," he began. "I could never go back to sleep, so I'd go to the breakfast room to make some waffles, and—"

"They had *waffles*?" I interrupted, outraged.

Oscar looked like he was trying not to laugh. "Yeah, but they were always out of batter by the time you woke up," he said, and I made a face. "Anyway, once I was full, I could usually go back to sleep. I think it was maybe the second day you were here—I went down right before six, and your dad was in the breakfast room video-chatting with someone. I guess he didn't want to wake you up. And . . . well, I figured out it was your mom he was talking to, and she told him that she was engaged."

I pictured Dad alone in the breakfast room, laptop open, Mom on the screen. *I have some news.* A rush of anger flooded through me.

"Sorry," Oscar added, and I glanced at him. "I mean, it was an accident, just like you with Aunt Lidia's phone. But still. I'm sorry."

I nodded stiffly. "It's fine."

"Do you want your parents to get back together?"

I blinked, surprised at the bluntness of the question. "No."

"Really?"

"Really," I said honestly. "Neither of them was happy." I pressed my lips together. There was more to it than that, of course.

"Do you want to talk about it?" Oscar asked, his tone slightly mocking.

For a moment, I just gaped at him. Because he was smirking. Like this was funny.

Then I realized . . . it *was* kind of funny.

"You know, I really, really don't," I said, shaking my head. "At *all*. Why do people always think talking about something that makes you miserable is going to help?"

"Exactly!" Oscar exclaimed. "Maybe it'll just make you feel worse."

"Let's see." I cleared my throat. "Last April, my mom suddenly decided she wanted to go be a famous photographer, and she had to do it *alone*. So she ditched us and moved to Cincinnati. She's taken off twice before, by the way, but she always came home after a few weeks. This time she came back to town in June without even telling me, and now all of a sudden she's marrying some guy *who has a daughter*. Gee, saying that out loud helped a ton. I feel *so* much better now."

Oscar leaned forward in his seat, his expression earnest. "My dad used to own a chain of cafés. When I was nine, he got audited and they found out he had some sort of embezzlement thing going on. He basically stole a ton of money from his own employees. During the trial, his name was all over the headlines of the local newspapers every day, and they made him sound like a supervillain with all these stupid nicknames. And we have *the same name.* He was sentenced to ten years in prison, and I got called 'Bettencrook' for most of fifth grade." Oscar threw his hands up in the air, eyes wide in mock surprise. "Magic! Talking about it fixed everything."

We both started laughing. It was that uncontrollable kind of laughter, where your chest starts to really ache but you can't stop. A minute later, the door slid open.

"Everything okay back here?" Mi Jin asked.

I nodded, wiping my eyes. "Great."

"We just solved all our problems," Oscar added.

Mi Jin looked amused. "Glad to hear it, but could you guys keep it down a little? We're going to start filming again—we're just a few minutes from the city. And be careful with the preciouses," she added sternly, gesturing to the comics strewn on the floor before sliding the door shut again.

I reached down to pick up *Avengers.* "Do you at least get to visit your dad?"

"Yeah." Oscar grabbed his comic, too. "But I haven't since I got expelled. Don't really want to have that conversation."

"I don't blame you," I said, flipping back to my spot. "All of that happened when you were nine, and kids at your school were still giving you a hard time about it in eighth grade? Lame."

"What?"

"That's why you got expelled, right?" I glanced at him.

"Lidia said you were bullied—wasn't it because of what happened with your dad?"

Oscar's smile vanished. "No, it wasn't about that. I, um . . . got in a fight with Mark."

Frowning, I remembered my first conversation with Oscar.

I had a friend named Mark, too.

Had? What, is he dead or something?

"Oh. What, um . . ." I trailed off as Oscar buried his head in his comic. Whatever had happened, obviously he didn't want to talk about it. So I closed my mouth and went back to reading. I was curious, but we'd already talked enough. And after all, I hadn't told him about the Thing.

Some stuff just hurt too much to say out loud.

Talking about *not* talking about our problems actually did help in one way—all the tension between Oscar and me had pretty much disappeared. It was like we'd bonded over our mutual agreement to shove our feelings down and not talk about them, ever. Roland would probably have a lot to say about how unhealthy that was, but I didn't care. Telling someone about the Thing wouldn't make any difference at this point. The Thing was officially indestructible.

"Why do we have to completely unload?" Mi Jin grumbled, crawling back into the van. "Can't we leave some of this stuff in here?"

"Can't lock it," Jess said, grabbing a stack of tripods. "It's a prison van—two lock systems. The exterior lock keeps people in, the interior lock keeps people out. The guy I bought it from said the interior lock has been broken for a few years, so we can't stop anyone from getting in. That's why it was so cheap."

She headed back inside, followed by Sam, who was loaded down with several equipment bags. The drive through Brussels had been amazing—I'd never seen such opulent buildings, with arches and turrets and intricate carvings all lit up and golden against the purplish-blue sky. We'd passed some of the fanciest, most castle-like hotels I'd ever seen.

Our hotel was not one of them.

"Looks like my college dorm," Mi Jin joked when she noticed my expression. "Only with smaller rooms."

I grinned, taking the bag she was holding out. When I stepped away from the van, Oscar pulled me aside.

"What?" I asked, but he just shook his head. I watched as he checked to make sure Mi Jin was all the way inside the van. Then he grabbed the handle to the sliding door and pulled hard. The door slammed shut, and through the barred window, we saw Mi Jin spin around.

"Hey!" She tugged on the door, her expression confused. "What are you doing?"

"Exterior locks!" Oscar said. "Just wanted to test them out."

Mi Jin grabbed the bars, and made a face like she was screaming. Laughing, I pulled the Elapse out of my pocket. "Do that again!"

A minute later, Dad came out of the hotel and found

us in the middle of a photo shoot, with Mi Jin smashing her face between the bars, and Oscar pretending to pick the lock.

"That's enough," Dad said mildly, pulling the door open. Mi Jin hopped out, looking pleased.

"Send me those, okay?"

"Sure!" I flipped through the photos on my viewfinder. Several of them were pretty funny-looking. Hopefully the *P2P* fans would think so, too. I turned off the Elapse, and it promptly turned on again. "What the . . ."

WARNING! High Voltage

I frowned, holding the camera closer to my eyes. I'd almost forgotten the other time I'd seen this message—in Crimptown, right before I'd tried to take the photo of Sonja. But it didn't make sense. It wasn't like a camera could *shock* you.

"There's an Internet café over there," Oscar said.

"Huh?"

Oscar pointed across the street. "You could post those on your blog."

"Oh," I said. "How'd you know I was thinking about posting these?"

"Why do you think I locked her in there in the first place?" he replied, and I smiled.

"Dad, we're going to the, um . . ." I paused, squinting at the name of the café. *Ciel Numérique.* "Uh . . . whatever that says."

"Ciel Numérique," Oscar said. "It's French, I think . . . Which is weird. I thought Aunt Lidia said they speak Dutch in Belgium."

"Dutch, French, and German are all official languages here," Dad replied promptly, heaving a speaker out of the van. "Be back at the hotel by nine, okay? Not a minute later, and no detours."

"Okay."

Oscar and I headed to the intersection and waited for the light. "You speak French?" I asked him.

"Portuguese," he replied. "Sort of. My grandparents speak it—the only time I really use it is around them. Some of the words are similar to French and Spanish, though."

"That's really cool," I said, reaching for the door. "I—ow!" A thin, pale woman with dark hair and a haughty expression pushed past us.

"Excuse you," Oscar said loudly. Scowling, she glanced from Oscar to me, and her eyes widened a little. Shoving on a pair of oversize sunglasses, she hurried down the street toward the bus stop without so much as an apology.

"Rude," Oscar muttered.

I stared at her retreating back, hit with a feeling of déjà vu. "I've seen her before, I think. Did she look familiar to you?"

"Nope." Oscar pulled the door open, and I followed him inside. We found two free computers side by side and sat down. I powered on my computer and waited for it to load, thinking about the sunglasses woman. It wasn't until I saw the coastal wallpaper on the desktop that I remembered.

"The waterfront!"

"What about it?"

"That's where I've seen her," I told Oscar excitedly. "The

day on the waterfront in Rotterdam. I bumped into her and she dropped her camera. It was her, I'm positive."

Oscar opened his browser. "So?"

"So don't you think that's kind of weird that she's here now, the same time as us?"

He shrugged. "Just a coincidence. She's a tourist. Brussels isn't that long of a bus ride from Rotterdam."

"I guess." But something nagged at me. Closing my eyes, I pictured her: pale, pointed face, sunken cheeks, sharp nose, long, straight dark hair . . .

"Kat."

"What?"

"Look at this."

Leaning over, I stared at Oscar's screen, and all thoughts of the snotty waterfront woman vanished.

P2P FAN FORUMS
Do you believe? Think again.

Anonymous
"The most fraudulent show on television" is heading to Brussels to visit Daems Penitentiary. Fake lightbulbs are nothing compared to what they've got planned for this episode—after all, they know it'll be their last one. Desperate times call for desperate measures . . .

Maytrix [admin]
Anon, please set up an account.

presidentskroob [member]
what makes you so sure it'll be the last episode?

YourCohortInCrime [member]
Rumor is if ratings aren't up by Halloween, the show's getting replaced with that new vampire series. The Brussels episode will air on Halloween, so it'll probably be the last one.

randomsandwich [member]
don't forget the curse. even if the show makes it, this is Jack's last episode.

Anonymous
It's everyone's last episode.

AntiSimon [member]
You don't know that for sure. The preview of the Crimptown episode they released yesterday is already getting a lot of buzz. I think ratings are going to be good for that one.

skEllen [member]
SAM LOOKED AMAZING IN THAT PREVIEW!!! I CAN'T WAIT!!!

Anonymous
[comment deleted by administrator]

skEllen [member]
WHAT????!!!!!!!11!!!!!!!!!!1!! D:

YourCohortInCrime [member]
Whoa. Anon, I was on your side. But death threats aren't cool.

Maytrix [admin]
Post deleted. Sorry, all. Please keep an eye out for this troll and let me know if he pops up in another thread. I'm closing this one permanently.

"*Death* threat?"

Oscar frowned. "Why would he threaten anyone?"

"To cause trouble," I said in disgust. "Look—that post says it's my dad's last episode, and then Roland said it's *everyone's* last episode. And then he followed that with a death threat. The fans will definitely talk about *that*."

Oscar watched as I opened the forums on my computer and clicked CREATE NEW ACCOUNT. "Um, what are you doing?"

"Making a forum account."

"Why?"

Logging into my e-mail, I opened the new message that had popped up asking for me to confirm my *P2P* forum membership. "Because I want to post. I can't write about this on my blog since I promised Lidia I'd get approval first. But they can't stop me from joining the forums."

Oscar stared at me. "You're not going to say anything about Roland, are you?"

I ignored him, already typing furiously.

"Don't." Oscar shook his head, and I smacked his hand away from the mouse. "No, seriously, Kat. Don't post that."

"Too late." I clicked SUBMIT, then sat back in my chair. My heart was pounding like I'd just sprinted a mile. Oscar let out a long, slow breath.

"Roland's going to be mad."

"So?" I tried to sound indifferent. "I'm not going to let him get my dad fired."

Oscar grimaced. "I'm starting to think firing your dad isn't the worst thing he could do."

"Don't be so dramatic," I snapped, clicking back over to

my e-mail. "Roland's not actually going to hurt anyone. It's just stupid publicity stuff."

But I couldn't shake off a tingle of fear. And as I wrote a long e-mail explaining everything to Jamie and Hailey, I kept glancing over my shoulder, half-expecting to see a furious Roland barge through the doors at any second.

CHAPTER EIGHTEEN
STALKER IN THE CiTY

P2P **FAN FORUMS**
A Message for "Anonymous"

Doctor Pain [new member]
My name is Kat Sinclair, and my dad is the new host of *P2P*. Some of you have already seen my blog. I actually only started it for my grandma and my friends to read. But I'm glad you guys like the posts.

I'm a skeptic when it comes to ghosts, but since I joined *P2P*, I've honestly seen some stuff I can't explain. (I didn't fake that picture of the outline next to Lidia. I still haven't figured out what that was.) I'm going to keep posting behind-the-scenes stuff about Brussels and the Daems prison episode, and hopefully more episodes after that. I hope you'll share them with your friends and convince them to watch and decide for themselves what's real and what isn't.

And Anonymous, if you're reading this: The only fraud here is you.

BETWEEN traveling to Brussels and the creepy situation with Roland, I'd pretty much forgotten about school. Oscar and I spent most of the next few days in Mi Jin's room going over history lessons and math problems. With our minds full of death threats and impending visits to haunted prisons, focusing on something as mind-numbing as linear equations was next to impossible.

The Crimptown episode aired our second night in Brussels. Jess streamed it on her laptop, and I watched it in her room with the rest of the crew (minus Lidia, whose cold was getting really nasty). I had to admit, the episode was pretty freaky. The fans on the forum seemed to agree. So did Grandma, who'd e-mailed me an in-depth review a few hours later. But the best news came the following morning, right in the middle of a lesson on the Battle of Antietam.

"Ratings are up 20 percent from the last episode." I barely got a glimpse of Jess's freckled face before she hurried down the hall to the next room. Oscar and I stared at the door, then at Mi Jin. She blinked a few times.

"Good," she said at last. "Yeah, that's good."

Oscar and I shared a cautious smile. The response to my forum post had been insane—as of this morning, the thread was already six pages long. Most of them seemed to think I was either really brave or really stupid. But more important, there were lots of new members. More fans were joining the forums, which I figured had to be a good sign. And my blog post with the funny prison-van photos had gotten almost one hundred comments, most of them from people I didn't know (in real life *or* from the forums). "Anonymous" had been silent so far.

I was on my way to the vending machines for some celebratory candy bars when I heard Roland's voice coming from Sam's room. I paused outside the door, listening closely.

"How many e-mails has she sent you?" Roland sounded

angry—none of his usual sarcasm. "You promised you'd tell me if you heard from Emily again."

Sam's response was inaudible. I pressed my ear to the door, heart pounding.

"...how these things work, trust me," Roland was saying. "I'm telling you, Sam—she's coming back."

There was a muffled sound that I realized a second too late was footsteps. I leaped back as Roland yanked the door open. He froze, staring at me. I stared back defiantly, my face and neck suddenly scorching hot.

"What are you doing?"

"Snacks." I pointed unnecessarily to the vending machine at the end of the hall.

Roland stepped out of Sam's room and closed the door, still eyeing me. "Doesn't that require walking?"

I glared at him, then continued down the hall. When I got to the vending machines, I glanced back as he stepped onto the elevator. The doors slid closed, and I breathed a sigh of relief. *Well, that could have been worse.* Although my fingers still shook pretty badly as I dropped a few coins into the slot.

So I was right—Roland was bringing Emily back. All he had to do now was find a way to get rid of my dad. Slowly, anger began to overtake my fear. I gathered up the candy bars and turned around just as Sam stepped out of his room.

"Hi, Sam."

Blinking, he turned and saw me. "Oh, hello."

"Everything okay?" I asked.

"Yes, why?"

"I heard Roland yelling," I said brazenly. "He sounded mad about something."

"Oh, that." Sam's expression cleared. "It's nothing. Kat, has our ghost tried to communicate with you again?"

"Huh? Oh, the boy ghost." I shook my head. "No, why?"

"Just wondering." Sam gave me a vague sort of smile as he fished a few coins out of his pocket. "Let me know if he does, okay?"

"Sure."

I watched Sam head to the vending machines, whistling softly.

The next afternoon while Dad and the rest of the crew packed up to head to the prison, Oscar and I had a video chat with Jamie and Hailey. I couldn't wait to tell them what I'd overheard between Roland and Sam.

"We've only got fifteen minutes before we leave for school," Jamie told us. Next to him, Hailey yawned widely. "But we had to talk to you guys, because—"

"We found Bernice!" Hailey interrupted, beaming. My mouth fell open.

"What? How?"

"I was going through some of the older forum threads," Jamie explained. "Someone mentioned seeing her at the natural history museum when they visited New York. The museum's just a few blocks from where we live, so yesterday Hailey and I went after school. It turns out Bernice works there now."

"And she was there!" Hailey added.

Oscar's eyes widened. "Did you talk to her?"

"Yup. We asked her why she left the show, and . . ." Jamie paused, glancing over his shoulder and lowering his voice. "Sorry, thought I heard Mom. Anyway, Bernice didn't really want to talk about it, but we told her we were afraid your dad was going to get fired, too. So she told us what happened."

"Someone *threatened* her," Hailey said in a loud whisper.

My pulse quickened. "Did she say who?"

"She didn't know," Jamie said. "She said she got unsigned letters telling her to quit by a certain date, or . . ." He paused, glancing at Hailey. "Well, she didn't tell us exactly what the threat was. But obviously it was pretty bad."

"So Roland's sent death threats before." I shook my head in disbelief. "Did you see his latest 'anonymous' post on the forums?"

"Yeah, that's why we wanted to talk to you about Bernice." Jamie leaned closer to the screen. "You guys should tell someone. Your dad, Kat—and Lidia, too. I'm sure Roland wouldn't actually *hurt* someone, but still . . ."

"We can't prove it, though," I pointed out. "It's our word against his. If we tell them, I bet Roland will have a whole story worked out."

Jamie looked troubled. "Yeah . . . well, be careful. Especially at the prison tonight."

Oscar and I shared a glum look. "We're not going," I said, and Hailey let out a yelp.

"Why not?"

I shrugged. "Dad and Lidia said we'd be bored sitting in a cell all night—like this hotel is so much more exciting than a haunted prison. Really, it's because this episode is a big deal and they don't want us screwing it up."

Hailey sighed. "That's—"

"Jamie? Hailey?"

"Gotta go," Jamie said quickly, glancing over his shoulder. "E-mail us, okay?"

"Okay!" I got the briefest glimpse of his smile before the call ended. Feeling deflated, I turned to Oscar. "What do you think? Should we tell someone about Roland?"

He shook his head slowly. "You're right about the proof. Maybe . . ." He stopped, mouth open, gazing at the chat window still open on the screen. I turned to look, too, and my breath caught in my throat.

XXXXXXXXXXXXX XXXXXXXXXXXXX XXXXXXXXXXXXX

They filled the window, as if an invisible hand was tapping the *X* key thirteen times, space, again, space, again . . . I jabbed at the keyboard and the typing stopped.

I turned to Oscar, who held his hands up. "Not me," he said. "I swear, I . . . I have no idea what that was."

It's the boy ghost, I wanted to say, but it sounded too melodramatic. Still, I couldn't help glancing around the otherwise empty hotel room.

"We're heading out in about fifteen minutes." Startled, we turned to see Lidia in the doorway, looking more haggard than ever. "Kat, your dad wants to see you before we leave—I think he's in your room."

"Okay. Be right back," I told Oscar, then slipped past Lidia and headed to the elevators.

I tried to tell myself it was just a glitch, but the reappearance of the thirteen *X*s was too weird. I wondered if I would have time to tell Sam about it before they left.

I found Dad in our room zipping up his backpack, and decided a little last-minute begging couldn't hurt. "Please, please, *please* let us come. I swear I won't wander off."

"Kat, we already discussed this."

I crossed my arms. "Have you considered the fact that this means I'll be staying in a hotel all night with a boy, unsupervised?"

Eyebrows raised, Dad shouldered his bag. "Is that something I should be worried about?"

Instantly, I wished I'd never brought it up. "Ew, no."

"Glad to hear it." Dad started searching the desk, moving his laptop and shuffling stacks of paper. "Of course, I've already set up a curfew for both you and Oscar with Margot—she's the receptionist tonight. She's going to make sure you're both in your rooms by ten. Your *own* rooms."

"What?" I cried. "Dad, what am I supposed to do all night?"

"There's this thing some people do," Dad replied, grabbing his key card from under his binder. "They lie down and close their eyes and lose consciousness for a while. I hear it's called *sleep*."

"Hilarious," I muttered. "Come on, can't I at least—"

"Kat, stop." Dad turned to face me in the doorway. For

the first time, I noticed how exhausted he looked. "I'm not making you stay here because I'm worried you'll interfere with the show. It's because I'm worried about *you*. It'd be one thing if you could stick with the crew, but—"

"Let us!" I interrupted. "We won't get in the way, I swear—"

"It won't work." Dad paused, closing his eyes. "In fact, I'm starting to think maybe this job won't work at all."

My stomach plummeted. "What do you mean?"

"I mean . . ." Dad shook his head. "We'll talk about it tomorrow, okay?"

"Wait." I stepped forward, heart pounding in my ears. "Did someone threaten you?"

"Did . . . what?"

"Is someone trying to make you leave the show?" I said urgently. "You know all the fans are wondering if this will be your last episode—that stupid host curse. Are you getting death threats?"

Dad set his backpack on the floor, eyebrows knit with worry. "Kat, why would you think that?"

And everything came pouring out. I told him about Roland, the messages on the forums, the deleted death threat. "He's bringing Emily back," I finished. "He told Sam so, I heard him. Roland was behind the host curse the whole time, and now he's trying to make you leave, too."

Pinching the bridge of his nose, Dad took a deep breath. "Kat . . ."

"You don't believe me?"

"No, I . . . I believe you think you're right," he said, and

I snorted. Perfect. "Listen, tomorrow you and I are going to have a talk. Because while I appreciate you're trying to help, I do *not* appreciate you eavesdropping on people."

I couldn't believe my ears. "But—"

"We'll talk about it tomorrow," Dad said firmly, picking up his bag. I could see his cheek muscle starting to twitch, but I didn't care.

"And Roland?" I yelled. "Maybe it was wrong of me to eavesdrop, but isn't it kind of worse to send *death threats* to people?"

Dad grimaced, glancing down the hall. "Roland's not sending anyone death threats," he said quietly. "He found some recently in Sam's fan mail, and he's trying to figure out how to handle it. No, *stop*." He held his hand out when I started to protest. "Kat, you're just going to have to trust me here—I've talked to Roland and Jess about this, and I know more about it than you do. Get some sleep tonight, okay? We'll figure this out in the morning."

He kissed the top of my head, and then he was gone. Fuming, I marched over to the window and yanked open the curtains. I glared down at the parking lot, waiting. Soon the crew appeared, loaded down with bags and equipment. I watched as they packed up the van and drove off.

Checking to make sure I had my key card, I stormed out of my room and headed for the elevators. So Roland had a story worked out, just like I'd figured he would. I remembered him talking about Sam's obsessive fans when we first met, too. He probably wasn't even lying about the creepy mail. But what about Bernice's death threats? And

Carlos's forged exposé? That was all Roland. And I had no doubt he was going to try to make this Dad's last episode, too.

I was so caught up in my anger, it was a few seconds before I noticed the 6 button was lit up instead of the 3. Frowning, I jabbed at the 3 button, but it stayed dark. The elevator arrived on the sixth floor, and the doors slid open.

"Come on," I muttered, pressing CLOSE DOORS repeatedly. Finally, they slid shut. I tried the 3 button, then the 2. Nothing. The elevator didn't move. Just as I was starting to get freaked out, the 6 button lit up on its own.

Ding.

The doors slid open again.

Okay, then. Looked like I was taking the stairs back down to Oscar's floor.

I walked fast, feeling unsettled. Up ahead, a maid grumbled as she rummaged through her cart of cleaning supplies. A moment later, the round-faced receptionist walked out of the room next to the stairs entrance—Margot, I remembered. She said something in Dutch to the maid, who immediately launched into a long, angry rant. When Margot saw me approaching, she waved for the maid to stop talking.

"Hello," Margot said, switching to thickly accented English. "Did your father tell you I'd be checking in on you tonight?"

I nodded. "Yes, ma'am. We'll be in our rooms by ten." I glanced at the maid, and my eyes widened. "Oh my God, what happened?" Her hands and wrists were stained a dark reddish-brown, along with about a dozen rags piled on top of her cart.

"It's only hair dye," Margot explained quickly. "The woman staying in this room decided to leave us with quite a mess to clean up." She said something in Dutch to the maid, who nodded curtly, grabbed a few bottles, and headed back in the room. Then Margot smiled at me. "Lidia requested that I order you and Oscar a pizza for dinner. Just call the front desk when you're ready, okay?"

"Okay, thanks."

Margot headed to the elevators. The maid had propped the door open, and I glanced inside the room on my way to the stairs entrance. Then I did a double take and, checking to make sure Margot wasn't looking, stepped inside.

The room was a *wreck*. Inside the bathroom, the maid knelt with her back to me, scrubbing the tub and muttering what I assumed was every possible curse word in Dutch. The white tiled floor, the sink, the mirror—everything was spattered in what looked horribly like blood (although I spotted the box of hair dye on the counter).

But that wasn't the worst part.

The bedding was slashed. Pillows ripped open, tufts of cottony stuff torn out and flung all over the room. The comforter and the sheets were shredded to pieces, as were the curtains. Even the wallpaper had a few gouges. I shuddered. It looked as if someone had gone berserk, grabbed a knife, and tried to tear the room apart.

I'd taken only a few steps back when I spotted the binoculars on the desk.

A feeling of dread crept up my spine and for a few seconds, I wasn't sure why. Then I noticed the pair of oversize sunglasses, and I remembered.

The woman at the waterfront in Rotterdam. The woman at the Internet café here in Brussels. I'd bumped into her both times. She'd followed us here—she was even staying in the same hotel. And judging by the state of her room, she was pretty ticked off.

But something else was nagging me. I squeezed my eyes closed, picturing her pale, sharp face. Young but kind of gaunt, shadowed eyes, dark hair . . . that nasal voice . . .

I thought of the box of hair dye and suddenly, everything slammed into place.

Sprinting down three flights of stairs, I raced down the hall and burst into Oscar's room, breathing heavily. He looked up from his laptop, startled.

"What's wrong?"

"Pull up photos from the first season."

"Huh?"

Without bothering to explain, I grabbed the laptop and typed in the URL for the official *P2P* site. I clicked PHOTOS, then SEASON ONE, and scrolled down till I saw her—young, blond, lots of makeup. She'd lost a little weight since then and her face had hollowed out, but there was no question.

"It's her," I said softly.

Oscar looked thoroughly confused. "Emily? What about her?"

I took a deep breath.

"She's here."

CHAPTER NINETEEN
THE ROAD TO
THIRTEEN KISSES

P2P Fan Forums
A Message for "Anonymous"
Doctor Pain [new member]

Anonymous
[comment deleted by administrator]

Maytrix [admin]
Enough is enough. If anyone knows how I can get in touch with
the Brussels police, let me know. This creep has gone too far.

I physically couldn't stay still. Jiggling my leg, I leaned
against the receptionist's desk, clenched and unclenched
my hand, drummed my fingers on the counter. Margot
frowned deeply, cradling the phone between her shoulder
and her ear. I watched her hang up, then immediately
dial again. With every second that passed, the knot in my
stomach doubled. Finally, she sighed and set down the
receiver.

"No response from Jack or Lidia," she told us. "But I will
keep trying."

I turned to Oscar. "We have to go to the prison."

"How?" he said immediately. "Lidia said it's a half-hour

drive—that'd be a pretty expensive taxi ride. How much money do you have?"

"Not enough, probably." I thought fast. We'd already asked Margot about the woman who'd wrecked her room. Margot refused to give us her name, but as Oscar pointed out, Emily was probably smart enough to use a fake name, anyway. And while her hotel-room rampage was probably enough to convince police she was unbalanced, we had no way to prove she was going to Daems. Or that Roland was involved in any way.

But he was. Emily was dangerous. And if Roland was in love with her, well, maybe that made him dangerous, too. All I could think about was getting to my dad before one of them could hurt him.

"Can you add it to our room charge?" Oscar asked, and I glanced up. Margot gave him a quizzical look.

"Sorry?"

"Can you call a taxi and pay for it, and add it to our bill?"

"Please?" I added, jumping in before Margot could protest. "They won't mind—this is an emergency."

Margot's eyes narrowed. "Your father was very clear that you were to stay here."

"But it's an *emergency*," I repeated. "A real one. If we can't get them on the phone, we have to go to Daems."

"Then I will call again."

I suppressed a groan of frustration as Margot calmly picked up the phone. Oscar and I exchanged irritated looks as she dialed, listened, hung up, dialed another number, and on and on. Finally, she set down the receiver with a loud sigh.

"It's an emergency," I said again, firmly. "Look, if they want us to come back to the hotel, we'll just ask the taxi driver to bring us back. No harm done."

"We'd be back way before ten, too," Oscar added, pointing to the clock behind her. "It's not even eight yet."

Margot eyed him, then me. Then, to my relief, she relented and picked up the phone.

"Very well. I will call for a taxi."

I exhaled slowly. "Thank you."

We stepped away from the desk, and Oscar lowered his voice. "Do you have your camera?"

I blinked visions of Emily sneaking up behind Dad with a knife from my mind. "What? Oh . . . no. Should I bring it?"

"Don't you think your post about the psycho former host crashing the prison episode would look good with a few photos?"

I made a face. "You know, sometimes you can just say *yes* without getting all sarcastic."

When I returned to the lobby, the Elapse safely in my pocket, I saw a taxi parked along the curb. I hurried outside and waited next to Oscar while Margot spoke to the driver in rapid French. Judging by his expression, he wasn't too thrilled about whatever she was saying.

Finally, Margot handed him a note. He took it, giving Oscar and me a contemptuous look. "*Treize baisers,*" he mumbled, settling into the driver's seat with a scowl. "*Mon dieu.*"

201

He slammed the door. Margot smiled at us wearily.

"Cyril is your driver. He has promised not to let you out of his sight until you are with the adults. But he is not happy about going to *la Prison Éternelle*," she added. "Everyone knows about the haunting. He is . . ." She glanced at the driver's window and lowered her voice. "Chicken."

I snickered, but Oscar was still staring at the driver. "Did he say *treize baisers*?"

Margot nodded, pulling the passenger door open. "Yes. It's what some locals call the road to Daems. You know what it means?" she added with a wink. But Oscar didn't smile back.

"Yeah, I think so."

I waited until we were pulling out of the parking lot, then sighed loudly. "Well?"

"Well what?"

"What does it mean?" I said impatiently. "Tres . . . whatever you said."

"Oh." Glancing at the driver, Oscar lowered his voice. "*Treize baisers*. I'm pretty sure it means *thirteen kisses*."

"You've *got* to be kidding me," I said loudly, and Cyril shot me a dirty look in the rearview mirror.

We didn't talk much on the drive after that. Before long, the city was just a cluster of tiny bright lights behind us. The sky was that purplish-blue shade it gets right before turning completely black; a few stars twinkled around the sparse clouds that still hung low from yesterday's thunderstorm.

"Do you think Emily's there already?" Oscar asked at last.

I pictured her room, all slashed and ripped apart, and tried to sound calm. "Maybe. But even if she is, she and Roland are outnumbered. And—"

Suddenly, Cyril slammed on the brakes. Oscar and I lurched forward against our seat belts. "What's wrong?" I gasped, massaging my rib cage. Cyril muttered nervously and smacked the side of his GPS console, which had gone dark. The screen flickered back to life, a blue dot marking us on the map with instructions in French down the side.

Continuez tout droit sur la 13e Av

Tournez à droite sur la Rue de la Paix

Still eyeing the console, Cyril stepped on the gas again. When we started to turn right, Oscar grabbed my arm.

"Look," he hissed, pointing out his window. I leaned over and caught a glimpse of the two battered street signs at the intersection, which were sprayed over with graffiti:

A chill raced up my spine, but I tried to keep my voice light. "Thirteen *X*. Well, I guess that explains the nickname."

Cyril tensed up as we edged down the road, shoulders hunching, fingers clutching the wheel. Privately, I thought he was overreacting a little. Then Daems Penitentiary came into view, and my palms went clammy.

The massive compound loomed in front of us, made up of at least five buildings that I could see. The brick was so grimy and stained, it was impossible to tell what color it had been originally. Instead of windows, slits barely wide enough to stick your arm through marked the floors. A tower rose twice as high as the prison, overlooking the courtyard. And the entire thing was surrounded by an imposing wire fence—probably three times my height, with giant barbed coils along the top.

"Pretty," said Oscar.

"Looks like my old Barbie Dreamhouse," I agreed. We smiled briefly at each other, and I was relieved to see he looked as nervous as I felt.

Because the truth was, Daems was the most horrific-looking place I'd ever seen.

When Cyril let out a piercing shriek and slammed on the brakes again, I nearly jumped out of my skin. The cab jerked to a halt, and Oscar and I stared at the GPS console. The map was gone, and two symbols flashed repeatedly on the otherwise black screen:

X <3 X <3 X <3 X <3 X <3 X <3 X <3 X <3 X <3 X <3

Letting out a stream of curses in who knew how many languages, Cyril threw the car into reverse.

"Wait, *stop!*" I yelled.

He shouted a reply in stilted English, his voice shaking. "I will not drive closer!"

"You don't have to," Oscar said urgently, leaning past the

front seat and pointing. "Look."

I squinted and realized with a wave of relief that the crew's van was parked not far ahead. Even better, the doors were open—maybe they were still unloading equipment.

Cyril hesitated, hands gripping the wheel. The hearts and *X*s were still flashing on the screen. Finally, with a strangled grunt, he threw open his door. "We walk. Hurry."

I scrambled out of the taxi, and Oscar and I hurried after the driver as he set off down the path toward the van. I couldn't keep myself from staring up at the prison, taking in every detail—the faded graffiti and large patches of dark mold spreading over the walls, the slits revealing the inky blackness of each cell, the tiny points protruding from the coils at the top of the electric fence, waiting to gouge and slash anyone who somehow managed to get that close to freedom . . .

It was horrifying, the kind of place that should have made me want to jump back in the taxi and get as far away as possible. But my fingers still itched to pull out my camera and take a few shots.

"Hello?" Cyril approached the van, casting anxious glances at the prison entrance every other second. There was a muffled response from inside, and my heart lifted. The feeling didn't last long.

"What are you two doing here?" Roland emerged from the van, staring from me to Oscar in disbelief, and my throat went dry. I glanced around him, but the van was empty. Cyril stepped forward and thrust something at Roland—the note Margot had given him. Oscar and I exchanged anxious looks as Roland skimmed the letter. When he finished, he gave us a calculating look.

"So what's the emergency?"

"Uh . . ." I glanced helplessly at Oscar. "I need to talk to my dad."

Before Roland could respond, Cyril cleared his throat loudly. "You stay?" he asked me pointedly, already taking a step back.

"Just wait one minute." Turning, I squinted at the prison entrance, but there was no sign of Dad or anyone else.

"They're setting up in the mess hall." Roland leaned against the van, eyeing me. "Something wrong?"

"I need to talk to my dad," I repeated. My palms were starting to sweat. "I'm not—"

"Hey!" Oscar yelled. I spun around to see Cyril sprinting toward his cab. We stared as he threw himself inside and slammed the door. The tires spun on the gravel as the cab turned in a sharp circle, leaving a cloud of dust in its wake as it sped back toward the main road.

Shaken, I exchanged a panicked look with Oscar. Roland waited to speak until the sound of the taxi's engine had faded.

"You two really shouldn't have come here. It's too dangerous."

I shivered, but managed to keep my voice steady. "I want to talk to my dad."

Roland nodded slowly. "All right, hang on. I just need to grab the extra flashlights." Casting a quick glance around, he hopped back into the van. "Stay right there."

My breath grew shallow. Reaching out, I touched Oscar's

arm and nodded at the door. He stared blankly for a few seconds, then his eyes widened in understanding.

Quietly, we edged closer to the van. Oscar pressed his hands to the sliding door, I grabbed the handle, and we yanked hard. Roland spun around just as the door slammed shut.

"Hey!"

I stumbled back as he tugged at the door, but the exterior locks worked just as well as they had on Mi Jin. Turning, Oscar and I left Roland yelling and pounding on the windows and ran flat out to the prison entrance.

CHAPTER TWENTY

THE THING 3: ESCAPE INTO THE ABYSS

Alarm: TAKE YOUR MEDS!

"OKAY." Oscar leaned against the metal double doors, breathing heavily. "That was dumb. That was really, really dumb. Aunt Lidia's going to freak out."

Smiling shakily, I rubbed a stitch in my side. "Yeah. We're so dead." Oscar half-laughed, half-groaned. Neither of us spoke for a full minute. I imagined I could still hear Roland, yelling and pounding on the windows of the van. Oscar was right—Dad was going to flip when he found out what we'd done.

Well, whatever. Saving him from a psychopath— possibly two—would be worth the punishment. Hopefully.

"Okay," I said at last. "He said they're in the mess hall. Let's go."

Oscar nodded. "Which way?"

For the first time, we took a good look around. Directly opposite the entrance, another pair of double doors was bolted shut with a rusted chain. The corridor extended to our left and right, both paths equally dark. Tiny patches of dim, gray light along the floor marked where the moonlight seeped in from the slit windows in the cells. Silence hung in the air like a heavy curtain.

Oscar and I edged closer to each other.

"Should we just yell? Maybe they'll hear us," Oscar suggested.

"What if Emily hears us first?"

He made a face. "Good point."

"So which way looks less creepy?" I asked.

"Let's see." Oscar squinted down the hall. "To our left, we have Serial Killer Avenue, and to our right is Rue de la Zombie. Coin toss?"

"Nah, easy choice. We can outrun zombies." We started down the hall on the right, arms bumping together as we walked. "Unless they're those really fast zombies," I added. "You know, the ones with superhuman strength that can run up walls and stuff. Of course, the good thing about them is they move so fast, we'd barely have time to feel scared before they were eating our brains."

"Thanks, Miss Sunshine."

"No problem."

Each time we passed a cell, I felt a chill—not from fear, but from cold. Somehow, the air coming from the cells was cooler than in the hall. We reached the end of the corridor and headed left, combating the oppressive silence with nervous jokes about vampire bats hanging from the ceilings and corpses in solitary confinement. I was describing my favorite scene in Grandma's fifth movie, *Return to the Asylum,* when Oscar stopped and grabbed my arm.

"Listen."

I held my breath. A distant *beep, beep, beep* was just barely audible over my too-loud heartbeat.

Oscar glanced at me. "The crew?"

"Probably."

We set off at a faster pace, and the beeping grew louder. When the corridor ended, we stepped into a small foyer. I scanned it quickly—a window crusted with grime, a dilapidated staircase, and a pair of doors propped open with mic stands.

"There." My voice cracked a little as we hurried to the entrance. But my relief didn't last long.

The mess hall extended in front of us, row after row of heavy-looking steel tables. Rusted, broken chairs were strewn in the aisles, legs bent or missing. A lone, battery-powered fluorescent lamp stood on the other side of the hall, surrounded by cables, bags, and other gear.

But the crew was nowhere to be seen.

"Perfect," I muttered, stepping back when a rat scurried out from under a table and fled into the shadows. "Just perfect."

Oscar groaned. "I just realized what that noise is," he said angrily, heading down the aisle. "Aunt Lidia's phone alarm. *Again.*"

I hurried to keep up with him. "For her pills?"

"Yeah." We reached the lamp and began digging through bags, looking for Lidia's phone. Oscar grabbed a backpack with more force than necessary, knocking over the lamp. I caught it, raising my eyebrows at him as I set it upright.

"You okay?"

"No." Furiously, Oscar dumped the contents of another bag on the table. "You've seen how awful she looks lately. She keeps forgetting her pills—it's not like her. Jess is making us go home for a few weeks after this episode so she can rest."

"Well, that's a good thing, right?" I asked tentatively. "She needs to get better. And you'll come back."

"Yeah." Oscar shoved aside a few folders and a walkie-talkie. "But if we go home, I'll have to visit my dad. And if I visit my dad, I'll have to tell him why I got expelled. And I—I just can't. *Ha.*" Oscar slammed the bottle of pills on the table with a sort of savage triumph.

Glancing at him, I unzipped a small pocket on the outside of a dark green backpack. "Here's her phone." I swiped the alarm off. "No reception."

Slowly, Oscar started stuffing everything back into the backpack. I took a deep breath.

"I know how you feel," I said. "I can't go back to Chelsea, either."

"Because you're mad at your mom for getting remarried?"

"No." I squeezed Lidia's phone. "Well, yes. But it's not just that. When she went to Cincinnati, I figured she'd either come back like she did the first few times, or finally focus on her photography, like she kept saying she wanted. But now she's marrying some guy, and he has a—a *daughter*, and . . ."

My throat tightened. Oscar quietly stacked the folders and slid them back into the backpack. I took a deep breath.

211

"The thing is . . ."

The Thing. I never said it out loud, not to Trish or Mark or Dad or Grandma. Because I knew how they'd respond.

Your mom loves you, Kat.

"She loves me," I whispered. "But she doesn't *like* me. Everything I do disappoints her."

That's not true.

"The first time she took off, I believed her when she said it was to give a real photography career a shot."

And she changed her mind. She came back.

"But photography had nothing to do with it. The real reason she left is . . ."

Don't say it!

But the Thing finally broke loose.

". . . me."

For a split second, I thought I saw a shadow flicker near the entrance. Not rat-size. Human-size.

"I used to think maybe she just never wanted kids at all," I said, still gazing at the entrance. "She's always trying to change how I dress, what I eat, everything. She'd *hate* my hair like this." I touched the back of my head self-consciously. "But it's not that she never wanted a daughter. It's that I wasn't the daughter she wanted. That's why she kept leaving. And now she's getting married again—and she'll have a stepdaughter. Elena." I closed my eyes. "Mom seems to like *her* just fine."

For the first time ever, I saw the Thing clearly, face-to-face. It had my eyes and nose and mouth, my old, long braid hanging down its back. It wore a pretty sundress, no Crypt

212

Keeper in sight. It preferred fashion magazines to horror movies, and shopping to paintball. The Thing was exactly what my mother wanted.

The opposite of me.

"I'm sorry."

I blinked, startled. "What?"

"Sorry about your mom," Oscar said again, staring at the walkie-talkie in his hands.

"Oh." I let out a shaky laugh. "*Sorry.* That's it? Aren't you supposed to say, 'That's not true, she's your mother and she loves you no matter what, blah blah blah'?"

Oscar lifted a shoulder. "Maybe you're right, though. Maybe some parents just—"

Creeeak.

We both jumped, staring around the mess hall. I stepped away from the fluorescent lamp and tripped a little on a roll of cables. No movement, no sounds . . . but I had the overwhelming sensation someone was watching.

"We need to find Lidia," I whispered.

Oscar stuffed the bottle of pills in his pocket before picking up the walkie-talkie. "Lidia?"

Nothing. Flipping the dial, he tried a few more times. "I don't know which channel they're using."

"Keep trying while we look for them," I said, itching to leave. The mess hall was creeping me out.

We crept toward the entrance, arms pressed together. I half-expected a pair of hands to shoot out from under every table and grab our ankles. But we reached the foyer safely.

"Back the way we came, or upstairs?" Oscar asked.

I studied the rickety staircase. "Not upstairs. Let's try to find the courtyard."

We hurried back down the dark corridor, both of us glancing over our shoulders every other second. Oscar kept flipping channels on the walkie-talkie, listening for the crew. Goose bumps broke out on my arms—the temperature in the hall was dropping. The Thing was right on my heels. I could sprint for hours and I'd never outrun it.

"Oscar?"

"Yeah?"

"Why can't you tell your dad you got expelled for fighting?"

Oscar didn't respond right away, and I wondered if I should've kept my mouth shut. Then he sighed.

"Because he's going to ask why Mark and I got in a fight in the first place."

I squeezed Lidia's phone again, my eyes darting into each shadow-filled cell we passed. I couldn't shake the feeling that we were being watched. "So, why did you?"

"Because . . ." Oscar hesitated. "He was my best friend, right?"

"Right."

"Well, I . . . I liked him. And I told him, and he . . . kind of freaked out. And told *everyone*. And—"

"Wait, told everyone what?" I interrupted, confused. "That you liked . . ." I trailed off as I realized what he meant.

Not liked him. *Liked* him. A crush.

"Oh. Okay," I said. Oscar glanced at me uncertainly, and I tried to smile in a reassuring way. "So—"

Beep! Beep! Beep!

I gasped, nearly dropping Lidia's phone. Oscar leaned closer and we stared at the screen.

KEEP HER AWAY <3 KEEP HER AWAY <3 KEEP HER AWAY <3

The beeps bounced off the stone walls, unnaturally loud in the tomblike prison. Frantically, I pressed a bunch of buttons at random. Oscar grabbed it and popped the batteries out, and the beeping stopped.

"Okay, seriously," he said. "What's going on? The phone, the GPS in the taxi, the laptop . . ."

"It's the show's ghost. He likes me."

He stared at me. "I honestly can't tell if you're kidding, Kat."

"Neither can I," I said wryly. "Look, Sam said the ghost of a boy haunts the show. The one in the photo next to Lidia, remember?"

I started walking again, and Oscar kept up at my side. "Oookay . . . so what are these messages about? *Keep her away* . . . Who's *her*? Emily?"

"I guess . . ." I trailed off, picturing the way the ghost boy had reached for Lidia as she'd crumpled. Ever since we'd left Crimptown, he'd been trying harder and harder to tell me something. And Lidia had been getting sicker and sicker. "No. It's about Lidia."

"What? Why?"

We passed the entrance and headed down the other hall. "The most haunted show on television," I said, thinking out loud. "It started with the dead air in the first episode—the séance. What if the show is haunted because the ghost from the lighthouse never left?"

The corridor dead-ended, another hall stretching out to our right. "Lidia passed out at the first séance, when the lightbulb exploded," I continued. "And then again in Crimptown—and she'd been with Sam right before that. The message says *the medium*. It's not that Sam is dangerous, it's that he contacts ghosts. He contacted the lighthouse ghost, he contacted Sonja . . ."

I stopped again, and Oscar faced me. "What?"

"Sonja *possessed* Lidia," I whispered. "Mi Jin said it takes a ton of energy for a ghost to possess a person or objects . . . but ghosts can manipulate *electricity*."

Oscar glanced down at Lidia's smartphone. "So?"

"The hearts," I said softly. "Her heart—*Lidia's heart*."

"What do you . . . ?" Oscar trailed off, and I saw the realization dawn on his face before I said it out loud.

"Her pacemaker. That's why they can possess her."

Oscar exhaled loudly. The temperature had dropped so low, I could see a wisp of his breath. "Okay. And now she's running around a prison with hundreds of ghosts. Perfect."

We walked toward the end of the hall, neither of us speaking. I was so lost in my thoughts about Lidia that we were almost in front of the last cell before I heard the rhythmic *scrape-scrape-scrape*.

Abandoning all pretense, I grabbed Oscar's hand. We exchanged a terrified look before taking the last few steps and peering inside the dark cell. A filthy cot was bolted to the wall on the right, directly below the sad excuse for a window letting in a weak ray of moonlight.

But my eyes went straight to the figure crouched in the corner, scraping at the floor.

CHAPTER TWENTY—ONE
THE RETURN OF
RED LEER

P2P WIKI
Entry: "Cold Spots"
[Last edited by beautifulgollum]
Cold spots are various spots in a haunted location with cooler temperatures, often thought to indicate the presence of ghosts which have not materialized.

MY skin felt like ice. All my instincts screamed at me to run, but my feet were frozen to the ground. It was a woman—a woman with long hair hanging in her eyes, head bowed, sliding something over a board lying on the ground . . . a board with letters, numbers, and a tiny light flashing red . . .

Oscar squeezed my hand so hard I cringed. "Aunt Lidia?"

My knees nearly buckled in relief. He was right—it was Lidia, crouched over Mi Jin's Ouija board. But she didn't stop moving the planchette when Oscar said her name. He approached her slowly, letting go of my hand to kneel down next to her. "Can you hear me?"

Scrape-scrape-scrape.

"You forgot your medicine again." Tentatively, Oscar touched her arm. I stared down at the board, a chill of dread slowly creeping down my spine.

"Oscar . . ."

"Look, it's right here." Oscar handed me the walkie-talkie and pulled the bottle of pills out of his pocket. "Aunt Lidia, can you stop for a second, please?"

"*Oscar.*"

"What?"

I pointed at the board. "Look at what she's spelling."

FREETHEMEN—FREETHEMEN—FREETHEMEN

"Free the men?" Oscar glanced nervously at Lidia. "What's that supposed to mean?"

I swallowed. "Remember the Ouija board? *Gather the women.* And the other one—*free them.*"

"So?"

"Oscar, think about it." My voice cracked with fear. "She's been sick ever since Crimptown."

"Yeah . . ." Oscar stood slowly, lowering his voice. "Wait. You think Sonja is still possessing her?"

"Not Sonja." Kneeling down, I grabbed both of Lidia's hands with mine. The scraping stopped, and suddenly the cell felt too quiet. Lidia didn't look up, though I could see her shoulders rise and fall with each quick, shallow breath.

"Who are you?" I whispered, then let go of her hands. I knew the name she would spell before the planchette slid over to the first letter.

REDLEER

The scraping stopped. Oscar and I backed away as Lidia lifted her head. Slowly, her lips stretched into a wide, wide smile.

But not Lidia's smile.

She lurched forward, shoving us aside with freakish strength. I slammed into the wall as Lidia burst out of the cell and took off down the corridor.

"Wait!" Oscar struggled to his feet and sprinted after her. Dizzy, I stumbled out after him. Tiny spots of light danced in my vision as I ran down the dark corridor. I could just make out Lidia racing around the corner, and Oscar put on a burst of speed. When a shadow lunged at him from one of the cells, I shouted a warning a second too late. The mess-hall chair slammed into Oscar's head with a sickening sound.

THUD.

I screamed as Oscar crumpled to the ground. His attacker tossed the chair aside, then stepped over his motionless body and walked toward me. Terrified, I stood rooted to the spot, unable to focus on anything other than the glint of the knife in her hand.

Emily Rosinski smiled at me. "Hello, Kat."

Without waiting for a response—my vocal cords seemed to have seized up, anyway—she grabbed my arm. I tried to call Oscar's name, but all that came out was a small, strangled cry as she pulled me past his body and down the corridor. Even in the dark, I could see a giant lump already forming on his forehead.

Emily's nails dug into my arm, and I winced. She pushed through a set of double doors, and I stumbled half a step behind her, dimly aware that we were outside. I was so fixated on the knife swinging back and forth at her side, several seconds passed before I realized I was still holding the walkie-talkie. I couldn't call for help now, of course—no one could get to us in time. Glancing at Emily, I tucked it into my jacket pocket. We crossed a small, walled courtyard, heading straight for the guard tower.

"Hope you brought your camera!" Emily said cheerfully, kicking the door open. The DO NOT ENTER sign fell to the ground. "This'll make quite a post."

The steep staircase twisted like a snake inside the tower structure, just wide enough for one person. Emily nudged me forward. "Up you go."

Weak with fear, I began to climb, Emily right on my heels. I glanced down every other second, my eyes seeking out the knife. By the time I reached the top, my legs burned and my heart hammered wildly in my ears. I hurried to the railing and stared down at the compound. The electric fence cast a long, jagged shadow that circled the courtyard. And there, huddled right outside the entrance to the main building with the rest of the crew, was Dad.

My knees nearly buckled with relief. I opened my mouth to yell for help and felt cool metal press against my neck.

"Don't interrupt," Emily said softly. "They're filming."

After a few seconds, she pulled the knife away. My breath came out in a shaky whoosh, and I gripped the railing until my knuckles were white.

This wasn't the fun kind of horror. This was really, truly horrifying.

I could barely make out Dad's voice as he slowly walked backward in front of Jess, her camera up and filming. Sam drifted along next to them, while Mi Jin trailed behind, glancing over her shoulder every few seconds. Probably wondering about Roland and Lidia, I realized, and almost laughed at the hopelessness of the situation. Roland was locked in the van, Lidia was possessed and doing who knew what, I was stuck in a tower with a lunatic, and Oscar . . . I felt sick when I remembered the way we'd left him lying unconscious.

"Almost midnight," Emily whispered, her gaze locked on the crew. "The fans will love this, won't they? Another host, gone. The curse continues." Grabbing my wrist, she tugged me over to a grime-covered control panel with a single, rusty lever. "Bunch of morons. You figured it out, though."

Confused and terrified, I watched her examine the lever. "Figured what out . . . ? That Roland got rid of all the hosts?"

Emily's eyes widened almost comically. "*Roland?*"

"Well, y-yeah," I stammered. "He got you fired, he framed Carlos with that exposé, he sent Bernice death threats . . ." I trailed off as Emily started giggling, a high, tinkling sound that made the hairs on my arms stand on end.

"Well, at least you got the first part right," she tittered. "Roland couldn't stand that Sam and I were in love. He told Jess I was unstable. Unstable! Can you believe the nerve?" Eyeing the knife in her hand, I decided now wasn't the time to be a smart aleck. "So Lidia fired me. And after I kept her secret, too! But I promised Sam I would come back. *I* set Carlos up, *I* sent Bernice those letters. I *made* this 'the most haunted show on television'—the host curse was all because of me." Emily slammed the knife down on the console. "Just one more host left to get rid of, right, Kat?"

Before I could respond, she grabbed the lever and pulled hard. I covered my ears at the resulting *screech*. When I lowered my arms, the air vibrated with a soft, deep hum.

"What . . ." I stopped, a jolt of terror ripping through me. "Did you just turn on the fence?"

"Your dad could use a few tips on being a real reporter," Emily told me, pulling out her phone. "After he interviewed that tourism-board member yesterday, I followed her to a bar and bought her a drink. Just talking about Daems had her all worked up. She told me—in the strictest confidence, of course—that even the city officials are so superstitious about this place, they never deactivated the fence. They think it keeps the ghosts in. Isn't that funny?"

Giggling, Emily held up her phone and started to record a video. "It's going to be an exciting episode, Kat. We should get a little extra footage. Don't," she added warningly when I stepped up to the railing. Dad and the others were crossing the courtyard, still filming, slowly making their way toward the fence. I spun around to face Emily.

"They don't know it's on!"

She snickered. "That's kind of the point, isn't it?"

"But—but what if Sam touches it?" I said frantically. "You don't want him to die, do you?"

Anger flashed in Emily's eyes. "He stopped responding to my e-mails. All he cares about is communicating with the dead," she snapped. "He might as well be one of them."

Okay, Roland was right. Total nutjob.

Without giving myself time to think about what a dumb move it was, I smacked the knife out of Emily's hand. It clattered across the floor toward the edge, and she dove after it with a cry, dropping her phone. I seized the lever and yanked as hard as I could.

It wouldn't budge.

"Come on, come *on*," I said frantically, throwing all my weight into it. But the lever was jammed.

Emily scooped up the knife and spun around just as I grabbed her phone. I lunged for the staircase, taking the steps two at a time without looking back to see if she was following.

CHAPTER TWENTY-TWO
FLIGHT OF THE INVISIBLE PRISONERS

WARNING! High Voltage

I sprinted across the small courtyard, half-expecting to feel a knife slash across my back at any second. Bursting through the doors, I ran straight to the end of the corridor and took the first right, then a left, then another left. Finally, I slowed my pace and listened for the sound of footsteps. But all I heard was my own quick, shallow breathing. I was alone.

Any relief I felt at having escaped Emily vanished when I remembered the crew wandering through the courtyard, clueless about the live electric fence. Fingers shaking, I swiped Emily's smartphone on as I retraced my steps back to where I'd left Oscar.

"No reception. Perfect." I tried cramming the phone into my pocket, but there wasn't room. "*Oh!*" I pulled the walkie-talkie out as I hurried around the last corner. "Dad? Jess? Is anyone . . . ?" I trailed off, coming to a halt. Oscar was gone.

"Okay," I whispered. "Okay. Now what."

Emily's phone suddenly blared with sound, startling me so badly I almost dropped it. I stared at the screen in disbelief. A video had started to play. And not just any video.

"Are you ready?"

"Shh!" I hissed, pressing buttons frantically as the lighthouse footage played. But the phone wouldn't turn off. I glanced around, terrified Emily would hear it and find me.

On the screen, Lidia's eyes flew open. This was the same video that Anonymous—Emily, not Roland—had posted in the forums. Lidia stared right into the hidden camera, right at me. Then the bulb exploded, and the scene went dark until Roland flung the door open. I watched him hurry to Lidia's side, check her pulse, slump over with relief when she responded. He ignored Emily's question about the fake lightbulbs and ordered her to turn off the camera. But this time, the clip continued.

Emily pulled the camera off the tripod, her eyes glued to Sam, whose head was in his hands. A few seconds later, Jess burst into the room.

"Lidia!" she cried, hurrying over to the table. Sam lowered his hands, and Jess glared at him. *"You did it anyway, didn't you?"* she said bitterly. *"You tried to contact Levi. I told you she couldn't handle it."*

"Excuse me." Lidia lifted her head. *"It was my decision, not Sam's. I wanted to speak to my brother, Jess."*

"I know, but . . ." Jess's face crumpled. *"Lidia, your heart's not strong enough for this."*

Lidia ignored her and started to stand. Roland took her by the elbow and slowly, they shuffled out of the room. Jess and Sam followed, eyes downcast. Emily waited until they were gone before hurrying over to the hidden camera—the phone I was holding. Her hand stretched toward the screen, and a moment later, it went black.

I exhaled shakily. Sam had contacted Lidia's brother in the lighthouse. Lidia's brother, who had died when they were teenagers. Levi.

The boy ghost.

I looked up, half-expecting to see him, and just barely managed not to scream.

At the far end of the corridor, Lidia stood silently, glowering at me.

"Lidia?" My voice shook. "I want to help you. Can you hear me?"

Creeeeeeeeeak.

My breath caught in my throat. Lidia slowly raised her arms, and all down the corridor, each and every cell door opened as if attached to her wrists with string.

"Levi," I whispered desperately. "What do I do? I don't know how to *help her.*" Even as the words escaped my lips, images flickered through my mind like a slideshow. Lidia's eyes flying open as the lightbulb exploded, Lidia collapsing when I snapped her picture, Sonja's spirit leaving her body crumpled on the ground . . . the lights, the flash . . .

Strobe lights can trigger my seizures, so that meant no concerts or haunted houses. Not that that stopped me.

"Oh!" Cramming Emily's phone and the walkie-talkie into my jacket pockets, I pulled out the Elapse and held it up.

Flash.

Blinking, I could just make out Lidia slumping against the wall. I glanced at the viewfinder and sucked in a breath. Because Lidia wasn't the only person in the picture. In front of each cell was the outline of a man.

The prisoners were free.

At the end of the hall, Lidia pulled herself up and fled around the corner. A chill blew through the hall after her as the ghosts followed.

I raced down the corridor and turned the corner just as Lidia burst through a set of doors. The courtyard—Red Leer was leading the ghosts to the courtyard to make their escape. The electric fence couldn't hurt a ghost.

But it would kill Lidia.

I burst through the doors into the courtyard, my lungs aching. I might be able to save Lidia from Red Leer. But not if she reached the fence first.

Distant shouts reached my ears, and I squinted across the expansive field. For a moment, everything seemed to move in slow motion as I took in the scene.

Lidia, running flat out for the fence. Jess, throwing her camera aside and sprinting after her from the opposite end of the courtyard, Dad right on her heels.

Sam backing up to the fence near the entrance as Emily approached him, knife in hand.

"*The fence!*" I shouted at him. "*The fence is on!*" But I was still too far away. No matter how fast I ran, there was no way I could reach Sam in time. But I was much closer to Lidia than the others.

My leg muscles screamed in protest as I tore after her. She'd nearly reached the fence, but I was closing in. A shriek almost caused me to trip, and for one horrible moment, I was positive Sam had been electrocuted. Then movement to my right caught my eye, and I glanced over just as Roland tackled Emily.

Relief washed over me, and I put on another burst of speed. Three yards to go, two, one . . . I grabbed Lidia around the waist and we both fell to the ground with an impact that knocked the wind out of me.

She rolled over with unnatural speed, but I managed to hold her down. My elbow stung, and I felt blood trickling down my arm. Struggling to pin her with one arm, I aimed the camera at her face.

"*Let me go.*" The low, growling voice wasn't Lidia's any more than the grotesque smile twisting her lips.

"I'm trying to," I gasped. Then I pressed the shutter button and held it down.

Lidia's eyes rolled back in her head as the flash pulsed like a strobe light, and her body went limp. Through the neon spots dancing in my vision, I glimpsed the hulking outline of a man with a curled mustache just before he vanished in a light gust of wind.

ERROR!
Cannot save images because memory card is full.

DANGLING my legs out the back of the ambulance, I watched through drooping eyelids as Dad and Jess talked with a few police officers. Next to me, Oscar sighed impatiently while the paramedic continued fussing over the lump on his head.

"I'm *fine*," he said for probably the hundredth time in the last hour. The paramedic rolled her eyes and, adjusting his bandage one last time, headed over to check on Sam.

"You were out cold," I reminded him, tugging the blanket the police had given me tighter around my shoulders.

"Yeah, but only for, like, a minute."

I offered him a section of blanket. Oscar shook his head just as a particularly chilly gust of wind hit. "Oh, fine," he muttered, tugging the blanket around his shoulders. Smiling, I scooted closer to him.

Dad kept glancing over at me, like he was worried I might disappear. After everything that had just happened, I figured he was mentally booking our one-way tickets home. I'd already told my version of tonight's drama to three different police officers. And it wasn't exactly a truthful version.

I mean, the part about Emily attacking Sam was true. The part about Roland wrestling her off him and getting a knife slashed across the face for his efforts was true, too. So was the part about Mi Jin pinning Emily to the ground and refusing to budge until the police arrived. And the part about Jess giving Lidia CPR and crying when she finally came to. And the part where Dad hugged me so hard I thought my ribs would crack, then promised I'd be lucky to be ungrounded before I was fifty.

But I didn't tell the police about Red Leer. My last decent photo was of Lidia standing at the end of the corridor, which was blurred with transparent outlines. The constant flash I'd used in the courtyard turned the pictures of her face into a warped, overexposed mess. I thought about how it would sound if I explained the whole thing to the cops: *Well, she's been possessed by the ghost of a pirate we picked up back in Rotterdam, and he tried to use her to free all the ghosts of the prisoners here at Daems. Luckily, Lidia's dead brother helped me save her with my camera.*

I figured that would just convince the police I had some sort of head injury, so I kept it to myself. But the *P2P* fans were going to hear all about it in my next blog post.

Which honestly would probably be my *last* blog post.

"Hanging in there, you two?"

Oscar and I looked up, startled. Roland smiled, then winced and touched the bandage stretched along his cheek.

"I keep forgetting about this thing."

"How bad is it?" I asked, holding out my arm. "Because I think I lost a few layers of skin on my elbow. It's pretty epic."

Roland chuckled. "Mine's a shallow cut. Although they said it might scar."

"Scars are cool," I assured him. "Um . . . I'm sorry about, you know . . ."

"Locking me in a van with a psychopath running around?"

"Well, yeah," I admitted. To my relief, Roland looked amused.

"You really thought it was me pulling all that host-curse garbage?" he asked, and I nodded. "Why?"

"Er . . ." I wrinkled my nose. "I thought you were jealous."

Roland's eyebrows shot up. "Jealous? Of what?"

"Well, that Emily was so obsessed with Sam. Because, you know . . ." I glanced at Oscar for help. He leaned away from me, palms flat as if to say, *Leave me out of this.* Sighing, I turned back to Roland. "I guess I thought you were in love with her."

For a second, Roland gaped at me. Then he burst out laughing.

I rolled my eyes. "Okay, so I got that wrong."

"A little bit, yeah." Roland shook his head, still grinning. "I've had my eye on her for a while, but believe me, that isn't why. She struck me as a little off from the very beginning."

"So you got her fired?"

"Yeah, but that was before I realized she genuinely needed help. And Sam . . ." Roland glanced over to where Sam stood a little apart from the others, his expression lost. "He's just clueless. I kept trying to tell him Emily's behavior was getting obsessive, but he didn't want to listen. Eventually, everyone but Sam could see it, and we fired her."

"When did you realize she'd set Carlos up?" I asked.

"Not until recently," he admitted. "Sam started getting letters from her again, and the writing reminded me of the threats that scared off Bernice. None of us thought . . ." His face tightened a little. "We didn't realize how bad it had gotten, or we would've done something sooner."

"Roland!" Jess called, waving for him to join her, Dad, and the policemen. One was still examining Emily's smartphone. I'd given it to him after deleting the dead-air footage. I figured there was enough evidence against Emily without it. Lidia didn't want fans to know about Levi's ghost, and the crew had kept her secret. I could keep him a secret, too.

"I guess it's my turn." Roland pulled a sucker from his pocket and ripped off the wrapper. "Not that there's much to tell, since I spent most of this whole ordeal locked in the van."

"I said I was sorry," I said, exasperated. "And besides, Oscar let you out eventually."

"Yeah, how about a thank-you?" Oscar added pointedly.

Roland crunched down on his sucker and, giving us an insolent look, headed off to join Jess without another word.

I glanced behind us, where Lidia was fast asleep on the gurney. I'd managed to get a few minutes with her before the paramedics arrived. She'd shown me the picture of Levi in her locket. He had the same sharp nose and amber eyes.

"Is he still here?" she'd asked sleepily.

"Yes," I'd told her. I didn't have any way to prove Levi was still here, but I believed it. As long as Lidia was near Sam—as long as she was a ghost hunter—she would be in danger of being possessed. And Levi would stay, to try to protect her.

So I would do what I could to help him help her.

"Thank you."

Glancing up, I realized Oscar was watching Lidia, too. "What? Why?"

"You saved her life," he said. "Thanks."

"Oh. You're welcome." It certainly hadn't *felt* like saving her. In fact, the way Lidia's eyes had rolled around in her head as I'd flashed the camera in her face would probably haunt my nightmares for a while. But it had worked— when she'd regained consciousness, she was herself again. Red Leer was gone. (*Where* he'd gone was something I was currently too tired to contemplate.)

"So . . ." I paused, adjusting the bandage on my elbow. "How long do you think you'll be in Oregon?"

Oscar made a face. "No idea."

We fell silent for a few seconds, swinging our feet over the concrete. I gave Oscar a sidelong look. "Think you'll visit your dad?"

His legs fell still, and he took a few seconds to respond. "I don't know. I guess so."

"Oscar, it'll be . . ." I stopped. *It'll be fine.* But how could I say that, when really I had no idea? Maybe Oscar's dad would understand when Oscar told him he'd been bullied because he liked a boy. Maybe not. Maybe my mom would start treating me like a daughter she actually wanted in her life. Maybe not.

"Whatever," I finished decisively.

Oscar's lips twitched. "It'll be whatever?"

"Exactly."

We smiled briefly at each other, then went back to swinging our legs and watching the crew.

Our last few days in Brussels were relatively quiet. I wrote a lengthy e-mail to Jamie and Hailey, detailing the entire Daems ordeal, and a much shorter version to Trish and Mark (after all, I'd be able to tell them the whole story in person soon enough). My blog post had a few hundred comments—some flattering, some insulting, but hey. As Roland had pointed out when he and the rest of the crew read it, the important thing was that people were talking about *P2P*.

Obviously, most of the buzz was about Emily's arrest. The forums had exploded with new members all looking for gossip about the former host and the way she'd sabotaged the show, all because of her obsession with Sam. Ratings for the Brussels episode were bound to be incredible, thanks to the media hype alone—even people who didn't care about ghost hunting would tune in just to see all the stuff with Emily. Fright TV wasn't canceling *Passport to Paranormal* any time soon.

And the host curse was officially broken. After a long discussion with Jess, followed by an even longer discussion with me, Dad had decided to stay with the show. But first, we were going back to Chelsea.

"The whole crew's taking two weeks off after the Brussels episode airs," I told Grandma, twirling the phone cord around my finger. "I think everyone needs a break after the whole Emily thing. But Fright TV is sending us to South America at the end of November!"

"Excellent!" Grandma exclaimed. "Does that mean we'll be having our annual Thanksgiving Freddy Krueger marathon?"

"Of course!" I paused, wrinkling my nose. "Unless you were planning to spend Thanksgiving with . . . I mean, I'll be with Dad, and I don't know if . . ."

"I'm sure we can work something out with your mom," Grandma said reassuringly, then yawned. "I hate to say it, but it might be time for me to hit the sack," she added. "Have a safe flight, okay? Tell Sam I said hello."

I laughed. "Not gonna happen." Hesitating, I stared at the laptop screen, where the *P2P* forums were still open. "Hey, Grandma?"

"Yes?"

I took a deep breath. "There's something that's been bothering me. I know the whole Sumner Stalker thing is just supposed to be a joke, but I . . . well, I don't think it's very funny. Emily . . ."

I paused, unsure of what I wanted to say. The truth was, Emily had terrified me far more than any horror movie or haunted prison ever could. I'd woken up at least once every night since Daems from nightmares filled with her high-pitched giggle, her hollow face, the gleam of her knife. She'd gone from being Sam's fan to something much, much worse, all because she couldn't let go of the bitter feelings eating her up.

"Emily was a real stalker," I finished. "I guess I just don't want anyone calling you one. Even if it's just a joke."

Grandma was silent for a moment. "You're absolutely right, Kat," she said at last. "I won't call myself that anymore. Or anyone else, for that matter."

I smiled, relieved. "Thanks."

After we hung up, I closed the forums and started to log out of my e-mail. Then I noticed my chat contacts list and, after a second of hesitation, opened the window.

MonicaMills [Mom]
Unblock this contact?

"Kat?"

I glanced up to see Dad in the doorway. "Yeah?"

"Lidia's cab is here."

"Coming." I clicked YES, then closed the laptop and followed Dad out into the hallway.

The whole crew had gathered in the lobby to say good-bye to Lidia. A few days of possession-free rest had done wonders—she still looked a bit drained, but much more like her old self. Still, Jess hovered around her with a nervous look, as if she expected Lidia to collapse again at any given moment.

I spotted Oscar standing off to the side as the others took turns hugging Lidia good-bye. He smiled when he saw me.

"Jekyll?"

I glanced down at my T-shirt. "Yeah. If I wear it inside out, it says *Hyde*," I told him, and he laughed.

"Nice."

"Thanks." I glanced outside, where Dad and Roland were loading luggage into the cab. "So . . . I'm going to meet my mom's fiancé this weekend. And his daughter."

Oscar made a face. "Well, maybe it won't be that bad."

"Famous last words," I said dryly. "If we were in a slasher movie right now, you'd be the first one the maniac attacked with a chainsaw."

"Probably." Oscar's smile faded, and he stuck his hands in his pockets. "I'm, um . . . I'm going to see my dad. Lidia said she'd set up a visit when we get home."

I nodded, unsure of what to say. We stood in silence, watching as Jess, Sam, and Lidia started heading out the entrance.

"I'm glad, though," Oscar said suddenly. "I'm tired of worrying about it, you know?"

"Yeah." I tried to sound optimistic. "And hey, the bright side is, no matter how good or bad things go, at least we'll see each other again in a few weeks."

"That's a bright side?" Grinning, Oscar dodged a light punch I aimed at his arm. "Just kidding."

"Oscar, let's go!" Lidia called, and he picked up his backpack.

"Good luck," I said, sticking my hand out. Oscar took it firmly in his, and we shook.

"You too, Doctor Pain."

Outside, Dad slipped his arm around my shoulders as Lidia and Oscar climbed into the cab. We waved until they pulled out of the parking lot and disappeared around the corner.

Roland stretched his arms over his head and yawned hugely. "I'm starving."

"Well, we've got a few hours to kill," said Jess. "Want to grab something to eat before the twenty-four hours of nasty airline food begins?"

"You should order the vegetarian meals," Sam told her mildly as we started walking. "The tofu curry I had on the flight to Rotterdam was delicious."

"It *was* pretty good," Roland agreed, exchanging an amused look with Mi Jin. "Probably because that was pork, not tofu."

I lagged behind, pulling my camera out of my pocket. Dad glanced over his shoulder.

"You all right?"

"Yeah." I waved the Elapse at him. "Just wanted to get some pictures, if that's okay."

Dad smiled. "Of course."

I slowed down, taking in the cobblestone street, the cluttered shop windows, the tiny tables set up under colorful awnings. Up ahead, Dad and Jess were chatting away about the architecture (judging from their animated gestures to the surrounding buildings), while Roland and Sam watched

Mi Jin drop a few coins into the case of an accordionist squeezing out an upbeat polka. For a moment, all five of them stood still as crowds of people hurried by.

Kneeling, I held the camera up to my eye. "Okay," I murmured, adjusting the lens until they were in focus. "Lots of motion around them, a slower shutter speed would give the crowd a really cool blur . . . wider aperture, shallower depth of field and . . . perfect."

Click!

1

Oct 10 • Emily Rosinski

Cannon Beach, OR • *Limerick Bed & Breakfast*

Creator and producer Lidia Bettencourt grew up in this coastal Oregon town, and her childhood fascination with the haunted lighthouse led her to choose it as the location for *P2P*'s first episode. The pilot episode included the infamous "dead air"—90 seconds during which viewers lost sound/audio. Fright TV could not explain the disturbance, leading to the show's slogan: "The most haunted show on television."

2

Oct 17 • Emily Rosinski

Seattle, WA • *Oxford Hotel*

The crew investigated room 610 of this hotel, where the ghost of a local author terrorized visitors by attempting to re-create scenes from her horror novel, *The Woman in the Mirror*.

3

Oct 24 • Emily Rosinski

Las Vegas, NV • *Burning Love Wedding Chapel*

This episode featured one of *P2P*'s most popular scenes, in which Sam Sumners attempted to contact the ghost of the Elvis impersonator who haunted the chapel and ended up entertaining the crew with a rousing rendition of "All Shook Up."

4

Oct 31 • Emily Rosinski

San Diego, CA • *Sandoval Studios*

This art studio claimed the spirit of a troubled artist haunted its gallery, occasionally making small changes to paintings, such as adding small clouds or extra stars.

5

Nov 7 • **Emily Rosinski**

Tucson, AZ • *Silver Rush Mansion*

The crew spent the night in this mansion, said to be haunted by the disgruntled original staff from the early nineteen hundreds.

6

Nov 14 • **Emily Rosinski**

Santa Fe, NM • *Dragonfly Dance Hall*

The spirit of a ballroom dancer betrayed by her partner lingers in the dance hall, occasionally trying to tempt visitors into a waltz.

7

Nov 21 • **Emily Rosinski**

Austin, TX • *The Asylum*

The crew investigated claims that this popular Halloween haunted house was actually haunted by a restless spirit year-round.

8

Dec 5 • **Emily Rosinski**

Dallas, TX • *OCH Recording Studio*

A fire claimed the lives of seven musicians at this studio over a decade ago. The studio was rebuilt and outfitted with new equipment, but occasionally, engineers report the song the band had been recording when the fire started begins playing through the speakers.

9

Dec 12 • **Emily Rosinski**

Lake Quivira, KS • *Crowing Farm*

The crew explored the cornfields surrounding this abandoned farm, once the ritual site for an eerie cult.

10

Dec 19 • **Emily Rosinski**

Madison, WI • *Stet News*

The owners of this local paper claim headquarters are haunted by the spirit of a disgruntled copy editor responsible for sneaking typos into articles just before the paper goes to print.

SEASON 2

11

May 8 • **Emily Rosinski**

Evanston, IL • *Saint John's Cathedral*
The crew investigates local claims that this church is haunted by the spirit of a young nun who tried to run away to enter a beauty pageant but was hit by a motorcycle and died on the front lawn.

12

May 15 • **Emily Rosinski**

Fayetteville, AR • *TW Hart Bridge*
Local legend says this bridge is haunted by the spirit of a bank robber in the mid eighteen hundreds, who sought refuge in the Ozark mountains and, when trapped by authorities, leaped off the bridge to his death.

13

May 22 • **Emily Rosinski**

New Orleans, LA • *Blacksmith Bar*
A fan favorite, this episode includes the infamous scene where Roland tries to conjure Bloody Mary in the mirror of the women's bathroom.

14

May 29 • **Emily Rosinski**

Charlotte, NC • *Dusty Wind Backcountry*
Those who venture out onto this difficult trail sometimes claim to see the ghost of a hiker who perished in the backcountry decades ago.

15

June 5 • **Emily Rosinski**

Charleston, WV • *Pelotaid Factory*
The fire which raged at this factory half a century ago didn't destroy the building—but it did claim the lives of eleven workers, who still roam the facilities today.

16

June 12 • **Emily Rosinski**

Oakton, VA • *Frostproof Gardens*
The crew spent the night in a greenhouse haunted by what locals referred to as an "agent of darkness" responsible for squeezing the juice from its still-ripening fruits.

17

June 26 • **Carlos Ortiz**

District of Columbia • *The White Whale*

In the first episode with new host Carlos Ortiz, the crew investigates a popular club haunted by the spirit of a guitarist. Some visitors claim to see colorful auras when there's a guitar solo during a show.

18

July 3 • **Carlos Ortiz**

Baltimore, MD • *Clementine Cottage*

The crew explores the former home of a local poet who believed the spirit of his deceased wife remained with him as his guardian angel. Even after his death, locals claim her ghost still haunts the cottage.

19

July 10 • **Carlos Ortiz**

New Hope, PA • *Brew Ha Ha*

This café is famous for two things: its delicious fried rabbit sandwich and the spirit of the woman tried and hung for witchcraft in the sixteen hundreds, who now haunts its kitchen.

20

July 17 • **Carlos Ortiz**

Park Ridge, NJ • *Bottle of Jinn*

More commonly known as "the one where Carlos got a tattoo," this episode features a bartender with a supposed third eye whose bar is haunted by a genie-like spirit capable of granting wishes.

21

July 24 • **Carlos Ortiz**

New York, NY • *The Alcazar*

This elegant theater claims to be haunted by the spirit of its first producer, who expresses his dissatisfaction during performances by flickering the lights and causing prop malfunctions.

22

July 31 • **Carlos Ortiz**

Monroe, NH • *Sacred Heart Church*

Locals claim a particularly wicked poltergeist haunts this church's cemetery, raising blood and bone from the dirt.